Andy Buckram's Tin Men

ALSO BY CAROL RYRIE BRINK

Family Grandstand
Family Sabbatical

Andy Buckram's

Carol Ryrie Brink

Tin Men

Illustrated by W. T. Mars

The Viking Press   New York

For
Sarah Jane Brink
with much love

First published in 1966 by The Viking Press, Inc.
625 Madison Avenue, New York, N.Y. 10022

Published simultaneously in Canada by
The Macmillan Company of Canada Limited

Second printing, August 1966

Library of Congress catalog card number: 66–11906

Fic 1. Fanciful tales—Modern
2. Robots

PRINTED IN THE U.S.A. BY THE BOOK PRESS

Contents

Jelly in the Hair

When he began to plan his first robot, Andy Buckram was baby-sitting with his Cousin Eva's Dot. It did not please him to be baby-sitting, so naturally he thought of something more interesting. As a matter of fact, Dot was not pleased either. If Dot had been twelve years old or if Andy had been two, they might have had something in common. As it was, Dot wanted her mama, and Andy wanted to be at his home down the river tinkering with his tools or reading the latest copy of *The Boy's Popular Mechanics Magazine*.

But baby-sitting was the quickest if not the easiest way Andy had of making money, and he really needed money. He needed it for electrical cord and solder and hinges and rivets and flashlight bulbs and all sorts of things that an inventive boy finds useful.

When Cousin Eva phoned, Andy's mother said, "Now, Andy, if Cousin Eva needs you to stay with Dot tonight, you must go. You can put off calking and painting the boat until tomorrow."

"Mama, I wasn't going to calk and paint the boat today anyway," Andy said. "It only leaks a little, small amount. I'll row up the river to Cousin Eva's in it."

"All right, dear," Mrs. Buckram said, "and be sure to take good care of Dot. She's such a darling baby."

"Yes, Mama," Andy said, but he thought to himself that his mother had no idea what an undarling baby Dot could be when she tried. Nearly everyone believed her to be a perfectly lovely child, but she certainly saved her worst moments for Andy.

It was a long row up the river from Andy's farm home to the farm where Cousin Eva lived. But Andy did not mind it because he had many interesting thoughts to occupy him. First, he thought about his inventions, and, after that, he planned the campout which he and his father always meant to take. Unfortunately Mr. Buckram had so much work to do on the farm that he had never yet found time to go camping with his son.

"But someday," Andy thought, "we'll go, and, when we do, I'll have everything planned."

When Andy arrived at Cousin Eva's farm, her dog Tiddley came wagging and smiling to meet Andy. But Dot took one look at him and burst into screams of rage. She banged her heels on her high chair and slammed her toys onto the floor and roared, "No! No! No!"

"She'll be all right in a minute, Andy," Cousin Eva said calmly. "She can have a cooky, if she eats her soup; and she likes the pink pajamas with the little bunnies on them to sleep in. Be sure to give her her blanky. Good luck, dear boy."

"Yes, Cousin Eva," said Andy as cheerfully as he could.

It is true that Dot stopped screaming as soon as her mother and father were out of hearing. But she scowled at Andy all the time that he was warming up the can of Campbell's soup that Cousin Eva had left for her supper.

Andy rarely had canned soup at home, and this smelled very good to him. Mrs. Buckram made her soup with a beef or a ham bone and a lot of fresh garden vegetables, and it was excellent soup. Still, a change is often welcome, and, besides preferring canned soup for its flavor, Andy liked the empty cans.

Empty cans can be useful in a variety of ways. They are good for holding worms when you go fishing, and the large ones are fine for bailing a leaky boat. But even more interesting are the many mechanical things that a clever boy can build out of cans. Andy had made doorstoppers out of cans full of sand. He had made cowbells out of cans, with clappers which he fashioned from jointed wire and small stones. For his mother's birthday he had made her a hassock out of six cans fastened together and covered with blue denim. The only trouble was that on the farm Mrs. Buckram was so busy that she rarely had time to sit down and rest her feet on a hassock. Laborsaving devices were more needed on the farm than devices to help one rest.

Of course they had electricity, and Andy's mother had a vacuum cleaner and a refrigerator and an electric stove. But water still had to be pumped by hand and carried to the animals, and there were many other things which took time and hard labor.

Andy had helped a little by inventing a way to open the chicken house door in the morning when the chickens woke up and wanted to get out to scratch. He attached the door by a spring to a movable roost. When the chickens all went to roost at night, the roost was weighted down, and the spring held the door tight shut so that no fox could get in to bother them. In the morning, when the chickens flew down from the roost, the roost popped up and the door popped open and let the chickens out. This saved Andy a trip to the chicken house before breakfast. It was a small thing, but Andy felt proud of it. He was a very inventive boy. But he had not yet invented a way to get along with Cousin Eva's Dot.

Now, as Andy looked thoughtfully at the empty Campbell's soup can and wondered what he could do with it, Dot was looking at him and wondering what she could do to *him*. Just as Andy reached for a bowl to dish up the soup, Dot's shoe hit him on the side of the head.

"Ouch!" cried Andy, and Cousin Eva's Dot laughed

with the first flash of pleasure she had shown. She had a very odd sense of humor for a baby. Andy saw that she was busy taking off the other shoe, and he just managed to dodge it as he put the soup in the bowl and set the bowl carefully on the tray of Dot's high chair.

"It's good, baby," Andy said. "Look! Here's your little spoon. Eat."

Dot regarded him with round eyes.

"No," she said.

"Oh, yes," said Andy. "Yes, yes, yes!"

"No, no, no. I-da-wa-na," chanted Dot. "I-da-wa-na. No, no, no."

"Yes. Yes. Baby eat it," urged Andy.

"No, no, no. I-da-wa-na."

Andy filled a spoon and held it out enticingly. The next thing he knew, the bowl of soup was on the floor, slam! bang! splash! While he went after it, Dot reached out for a dish of grape jelly that stood on the table and turned it upside down on her head.

"Great frogs and catfish!" yelled Andy. "Can't you behave?"

"No, no, no. I-da-wa-na," said Dot delightedly. Her eyes looked very blue between the streams of purple jelly that trickled down her forehead and cheeks.

Tiddley, the dog, was most helpful in cleaning up the soup, but Andy had a terrible time getting the purple jelly out of Dot's yellow hair.

After Andy had cleaned her all up and put her into her

pink pajamas with the bunnies on them, Dot said, "I wa cook-ky." That reminded Andy that she had not eaten a bite of food. So he had to start all over again to open and heat a can of soup.

This time he took care not to leave anything that could be thrown or turned upside down on her head within Dot's reach. While the soup heated, Andy removed the labels from the soup cans, and washed the cans out to keep for future use. Sitting side by side, they looked to Andy like two short tin legs. By this time the soup was ready to serve.

"Good soup," said Andy hopefully. "Nice baby eat it."

"Cook-ky, cook-ky. I-wa-cook-ky," chanted Dot.

"No," Andy said. "Soup first, then cooky. Understand?"

"I-wa-cook-ky." Dot scowled.

Andy saw that quick action of some kind was required. If Dot's interest could be engaged in something besides soup, he might be able to get her to eat without her noticing that she was doing so.

Andy put the two first fingers of his left hand into the two cans and made them walk along the table like two legs.

"Look, baby," Andy said, "walky-walk."

Dot stared at the walking cans, and, when she opened her mouth to laugh, Andy popped in some soup from a spoon which he had ready in his right hand. Dot hardly noticed that she was eating soup at all.

"Oh, frogs and catfish!" Andy said. "Wouldn't it be wonderful to have a tin baby-tender? A robot sitter?"

The cans continued to walk and the soup to go down Dot's red lane, and Andy began to tell Dot all about the wonderful robot he had seen last Christmas at Cousin Charles Bedlington's house in Des Moines. She probably did not understand a word he said, but she ate her soup just the same, and she was on her ninth cooky before he finished telling her about Cousin Charles's robot.

Cousin Charles's robot was a small plastic man about a foot tall. When Charles plugged him into a socket, his electric eye bulbs lighted up and he was ready to respond to various push buttons on a control board. Cousin Charles could make the robot, whose name was Robbie, move

13

forward and backward, raise his arms, and turn his head. Robbie had come from a toy store, for Charles was not a very inventive boy, and his parents had plenty of money to buy expensive toys for him.

Andy wanted a toy like Robbie as much as he wanted to go camping. But he knew that, if he was ever to get such a toy, he would have to make it himself. His parents certainly could not afford to spend their money on expensive toys, even for their only child.

For six or seven months, ever since he had visited Des Moines at Christmas, Andy had dreamed of a toy like Robbie. But it was not until he made the two tin cans walk across the table to amuse Dot that he suddenly decided he would try to build a robot for himself. The idea excited him very much. He was sure, quite sure, that he could do it.

While she was eating her ninth cooky, Dot's eyes began to grow very heavy.

"B'anky," she said.

Andy knew what this meant. He put her in her crib and gave her a sad old piece of ragged blanket, which she pressed lovingly against her cheek.

"B'anky," she murmured happily. She put her thumb in her mouth and went right off to sleep. She did look like a nice child after she was asleep.

"Well"—Andy sighed—"that's the easiest time I ever had with her. The walking cans did it. The cans—the robot! Oh boy, oh boy!"

The house was nice and quiet now, and, leaving Tiddley in charge, Andy went out to the woodshed, where he found a pile of empty cans waiting to be carted away by Grandpa Clayton, the junkman who lived down the river. There were a lot of soup cans as well as cans of other sizes. Andy selected a two-pound coffee can for the body, a number-two Sultana peach can for the head, a frozen-orange-juice can for the neck, and a lot of Campbell's soup cans for the arms and legs.

When Cousin Eva came home, Andy asked her if he might have the cans.

"Why, certainly, dear boy," she said. "They are just waiting for Grandpa Clayton to come by and collect them. I'm very happy to be rid of them. And here is your fifty cents for sitting. Was Dot a good little girl?"

"Pretty good," Andy said. "But I'm afraid we used up your grape jelly and most of your cookies."

"Never mind," Cousin Eva said. "I can always make more. And here's a carton for your cans, Andy."

Andy put the cans in the carton and carried them down to his boat. The boat was named *Dorinda*, and it was very useful to Andy in getting up and down the big river. The only trouble was that it did leak, and somebody would soon have to calk and paint it. It had been leaking while Andy was baby-sitting, and he had to use the large coffee can to bail the inside of it before he could start to row home. But really it was very easy to bail a little bit every time he needed the boat, and Andy knew now that he would have to build his robot before he could possibly get around to calking and painting *Dorinda*.

To row down the river was much easier than to row up against the current. Now Andy had little to do but row gently and steer for home in the soft darkness. He had plenty of time to think. Already he imagined just exactly how he would put the cans together and wire and joint them for action. He could see it all as plain as day.

"I'll use flashlight bulbs for eyes and pulleys to make the legs work. My robot will be a real man, there won't be anything babyish or toylike about him. I'll give him a man's name, too. I think I'll call him Campbell," Andy said happily to himself. He felt so pleased that he began to whistle a tune. He had often heard the tune, but he did not even realize that it was, "The Campbells are coming, oho! oho! The Campbells are coming, oho!"

Campbell

It is not easy to build a robot, and only very clever boys should try it. A few years ago there was a piece in the newspaper about a thirteen-year-old boy in California who built seven robots, one of them six feet, ten inches tall. The boy's name was Alan, and, if he could do it, why in the world should not Andy Buckram do it too? The answer, of course, is that Andy did.

It must be admitted that Andy had a few difficulties in building his first robot. Who wouldn't? In the first place, he ran out of cans. It took two soup cans for each arm and a half a can for each hand. Andy used tin-cutters to cut the cans and he wired the arms so they would bend

17

at the elbow, and added the hands neatly. Then he attached them to the two-pound coffee can for the body. With the head and neck in place, Campbell began to look very much like a man. But, of course, the legs were going to be the most important part, because Andy meant his man to walk. He decided to use three soup cans for each leg, and a large can, turned on its side, for each foot. The feet would have to be a bit clumsy because they would have to contain the wheels and pulleys that would make Campbell walk.

At this point Andy discovered that he lacked one can. He looked all around the house, and finally he went to his mother and asked her if she had any soup cans.

"Canned soup?" cried Mrs. Buckram when Andy asked her. "Mercy no! I wouldn't have the stuff in the house, not when I can get a nice beef or ham bone and some fresh garden vegetables. However, I do have a tomato-sauce can that I emptied the last time I made spaghetti. You can have that."

Andy did not know what he had better do. The tomato-sauce can was a little shorter than a soup can, and to use it would make Campbell limp. Andy thought about going back to Cousin Eva's for the right-sized can. But he felt eager to finish the robot, now that it was so nearly done. To go to Cousin Eva's would mean bailing the boat, and rowing upriver against the current, and running the risk of becoming involved with Dot. Andy decided that a little limp never hurt any robot who was right in other ways.

"It will make him interesting, won't it, Mama?" Andy said to his mother.

"Yes, it will give him a nice homemade look," said Mrs. Buckram pleasantly. Coming from her, this was a compliment, for Mrs. Buckram loved home so much that she considered anything homemade to be superior to what you could get at the store.

So Andy went on working, and presently he had finished, all except screwing in the flashlight-bulb eyes and doing the electrical wiring. For the electrical wiring he had to get some help from his father. Mr. Buckram had become interested in Andy's project, and he gladly contributed what knowledge he had about electricity.

"But next time, Daddy, I can do it alone," Andy said as they were finishing the job.

"Next time?" said Mr. Buckram. "What do you mean, next time? You know very well that the next thing you have to do is to calk and paint the boat, Andy. Even if this thing works, which I very much doubt, you will have your robot. One robot in the family is certainly enough, if not too much."

"Yes, Daddy," said Andy absent-mindedly. He was looking at Campbell very critically, and thinking to himself that light-bulb eyes were not enough to make the robot look like a man. He needed a mouth and a nose and ears.

"I'll certainly have to finish his face," Andy said to himself, and he began to wonder what in the world he could use. Water colors and crayons would be of no use on tin.

They would not stick at all. What would? Suddenly Andy thought of his mother's pink nail polish, which she used only on Sundays when she went to church. That should certainly stick hard and fast to tin.

"Mama," Andy asked, "may I have just a little, small amount of your pink nail polish?"

"Well, I suppose so. But be careful."

It took more nail polish than Andy had expected, and making the face proved to be the hardest part of building the robot for Andy. He was a very inventive boy where mechanical things were concerned, but he had not had much experience as an artist. He worked a long time on Campbell's face, and, when he had finished, Andy did not feel completely satisfied. He could not quite tell what was the matter. He wanted Campbell to look like a man, but somehow the tin man looked like a baby. Why this should be, Andy could not imagine. Was it because Cousin Eva's Dot had inspired the whole business that the robot seemed to look like her? Or was it only that he looked like the Campbell Kids in the soup ads? The more Andy looked at him, the more Andy saw that Campbell had a kind of spoiled-baby look that did not belong on a tin man. Unfortunately, by the time Andy understood the trouble it was too late to do anything about it. The nail polish had dried hard and permanently.

"Well," Andy thought, "if only his wiring works properly, I'll try not to care how he looks."

In spite of the fact that they disapproved of robots in

general, Mr. and Mrs. Buckram had become very much interested in Andy's work. When Campbell was finished and Andy stood ready to plug him in for the first time, they were almost as excited as Andy.

"You don't suppose that the thing will really work, do you?" asked Mrs. Buckram.

"Mama, it's not a thing. It's a man," Andy said.

"Well, it ought to work," Andy's father said. "I helped to wire it, and the boy has put enough time into it, not to mention all the money he has spent on electric cord and gadgets of one kind and another. Plug your man in, Andy."

Very excited and nervous, Andy plugged the robot into an electric outlet in the kitchen and turned the control switch. Immediately Campbell's eyes lit up. He trembled all over, and for a terrible instant Andy thought that he was going to fall down in a clattering heap. But then the little wheels began to go around and the drive shaft to work the pulleys and the pulleys to move the legs.

"Oh, frogs and catfish!" Andy yelled. "He's walking! He's walking!"

Slowly and jerkily, Campbell began to limp across the kitchen floor. He headed toward Mrs. Buckram, and he looked so real and alive that she suddenly began to scream and jumped up on a chair, just as she would have if she had seen a mouse or a snake.

"Turn him off!" she cried.

"Why, Mama, he won't hurt you," Andy said. "He's only a tin man."

But Mrs. Buckram continued to stand on the chair with her skirt gathered up about her while Campbell walked toward her. When he had come quite close, Campbell tilted up his head, for all the world as if he were looking at her, and he held up his arms to her as if he wished to be taken up.

"Why, he's a baby!" cried Mrs. Buckram, coming down from her chair. "A darling baby, and he wants to be taken up."

Andy turned off the control, and Campbell stood still. The robot had worked faultlessly, and Andy should have felt nothing but pride and delight. But he had intended to make a man, and it embarrassed him to see his tin man behaving like a baby.

"Mama," Andy protested, "he's *not* a baby. He's a man, a robot, a tin man. I'm not surprised that he scared you."

"Scared?" said Mrs. Buckram. "Why, I was only scared for a minute before I saw what a sweet little thing he is. He's a perfect darling, with his limp and his pretty face, and holding up his arms to be taken just like a baby. He's so cute. I don't know how you did it, Andy." Andy did not know either. He felt disappointed and ashamed.

"I didn't mean to make him cute," he said. "I meant to make a man."

But no one could be angry with Campbell for long. It was too fascinating to plug him in and make him walk and turn his head and hold up his arms. Andy would have stayed indoors all day playing with him, but, of course, he had the usual chores to do. He left the robot in his room while he pumped water for the cows and pigs and fed the chickens and curried the horses.

When Mrs. Buckram dusted Andy's room, she found Campbell standing in a corner behind the door.

"Poor little fellow!" she said. She went out into the shed and found the little chair that Andy had sat in when he was three years old. She placed Campbell lovingly in it. "There, dear," she said. "You won't have to stand on that poor lame leg while Andy is away. Mama will look out for you."

"He could just as well stand," Andy said later. "He's really a man." But Mrs. Buckram was firm.

"He's only a baby," she said, "and lame, too, poor dear!"

There were two good reasons why Andy kept thinking about making another robot. One, of course, was that Campbell had turned out to be a baby. Except that he did not kick his heels and shout, "No! No! No! I-da-wa-na," and that he could be unplugged whenever Andy tired of him, Campbell reminded Andy too much of Cousin Eva's Dot.

"If I could build a robot that would act like a man, and do something useful!" Andy thought. That was the second thing which made him dissatisfied with Campbell: Campbell could walk and move his head and hold up his arms, but none of these things was really useful.

When Andy's own arms grew tired of pumping and carrying pails of water to the cattle, he thought, "What I need is a good, big strong robot. I need one that could carry pails of water and empty them into the watering trough. I wouldn't mind pumping, but if I could make a tin man who would carry the pails to the trough and dump the water in, that would be something."

"Andy," called Mr. Buckram, "get a move on, son. It

looks like you're daydreaming again. And after you water the beasts, you'd better see about calking and painting the boat."

"Daddy, the boat only leaks a little, small amount," Andy said. But he hurried up and filled the watering trough for the cows and horses, and the pig trough, and the pans for the chickens.

When he had finished all his work except the boat, which certainly could wait for a few days more, Andy climbed the hill behind the farmhouse to the old abandoned turkey house which stood under the big pine tree.

The Buckrams had never had good luck with turkeys, and now this little building stood unused. It had a few old axes and tools and extra oars and paddles stored in it on the dirt floor, but otherwise it was empty. The turkey house stood on higher ground than any of the other farm buildings, and it had a nice view out over the river and across to the other bank. The tall pine tree sighed in the breeze, and Andy found this a very cool and comfortable spot in which to do his thinking and planning. He used to sit here and dream about building a campsite in the wilderness, but now that he had built a robot he could think of nothing but robots.

So more and more, Andy left Campbell to sit in the little chair at the foot of his bed, while he went up to the old turkey house and planned and thought. With all the experience he had gained in building Campbell, Andy knew that he would be able to build a bigger and better robot.

"I'll call him Bucket," he thought. "He'll have hooks instead of hands, and on each hook I'll hang a bucket. He will be very large and strong, and I think he'll have to have a battery inside him, because he wouldn't be very useful if he had to be plugged into a socket and drag a long cord after him. I want him to be a real man and do some useful work for me."

This was all very well, of course, but where were large enough cans to be found? And a strong battery, and all the rest of the things that would be needed? Andy had spent nearly all of his savings on materials to make Campbell, and look what he had got for his money! A baby like Cousin Eva's Dot! "Well, he *is* cute, all right," Andy said to himself, "and I *am* fond of him. But now that I have imagined Bucket, I just can't rest until I have built him."

Finally a good idea occurred to Andy. Downriver a few miles was Grandpa Clayton's junkyard, and Andy knew it to be full of cans and pieces of tin and old batteries and large oil drums and wrecked automobiles and many other interesting things. Andy had often gone by the junkyard on the river when he floated downstream to fish. The sight of it always gave Andy a lift of pleasure. Here were many exciting possibilities to a boy with an inventive turn of mind. He had never stopped at the junkyard, but he felt sure that Mr. Clayton would have the things he needed, and perhaps they would not be very expensive.

Andy had a slight acquaintance with Sparrow Clayton, the old man's granddaughter. She was in Andy's room at school. But she was a quiet girl, and he had never really paid any attention to her. She was small for her age, and she always got her lessons without any fuss, so that nobody really noticed her.

When Andy had thought about Grandpa Clayton's junkyard for a while, he went down to the river and bailed out the boat. Just before he pushed off from shore, he suddenly thought of something else. He ran up to the house and got Campbell, wound his cord around his middle, and carried him down to the boat.

Campbell sat up very nicely in the stern of the boat while Andy rowed and drifted down the river to the Clayton place.

Graveyard and Spare Parts

Sparrow Clayton stood on the dock, trying to catch a catfish for dinner. Andy knew that her real name was Eliza Jane and that she was eleven and a half years old. But she scarcely looked more than ten, and she was so brown and perky that the nickname Sparrow seemed to suit her better than Eliza Jane.

"You get a big catfish on that hook, and likely it'll pull you right off the dock and into the water, and swim away with you," said Andy, as he pulled his boat in beside the Clayton dock.

"Oh, I don't think so," Sparrow said. "I've caught some pretty big ones, and I never got pulled off the dock yet."

"Is your grandpa here?"

"Yes, he's up at the Graveyard," Sparrow said.

"The graveyard?" repeated Andy. "I didn't know you'd lost anybody recently. I mean—" He suddenly felt embarrassed, because he knew that Sparrow was an orphan except for her grandfather, and he pictured the old gentleman laying flowers on a family grave while his poor little granddaughter had to fish for a living.

"I mean the Automobile Graveyard," Sparrow said. "Grandpa doesn't like for folks to call this a junkyard. He calls it the Automobile Graveyard and Spare Parts Lot. I think that's nicer too."

"Oh," said Andy.

"Grandpa says old cars deserve a good final resting place as much as people do—more, maybe, because they work so hard and run so fast and often get badly treated. People love their cars when they are new and shiny, but when they get old and rusty they throw them out and call them junk. Grandpa doesn't think that anything ought to be called junk."

"Well, I like junk," Andy said, "if something can be made of it. I like things to be useful."

"So do I," said Sparrow. She reeled in her line and laid her fishing rod down on the dock. "Did you come to sell something?" she asked. "I see you have some cans in the back of the boat."

"Cans?" cried Andy in a huff. "That's Campbell. That's my robot."

"Robot?" repeated Sparrow, puzzled. "What's a robot?"

"Well, he's a tin man," Andy explained. "Great frogs and catfish! Don't you really know what a robot is? It's a mechanical man who works by electricity. I built this one myself."

"Really?" said Sparrow. "What can he do?"

"He walks and turns his head and puts up his arms, and his eyes light up. Do you have an outlet somewhere, where I can plug him in and show you?"

"Yes," Sparrow said, "we've got electricity up to the house. Come on up."

She led the way up the bank by a narrow path between piles of the most delightful junk that Andy had ever seen. He kept stopping and exclaiming, "Old batteries! Oh, boy!" and, "What a whopping piece of tin!" and, "Gol*lee*! Buckets and oil drums!"

"May I carry him?" Sparrow asked.

"Who?" said Andy.

"Your robot," Sparrow said. Andy had flung Campbell over his shoulder and nearly forgotten about him in the excitement of seeing all the material he needed for making Bucket.

"Why, I guess you can," he said, "if you'll be careful of him."

"Oh, he's cute!" cried Sparrow, taking the tin man into her arms and holding him carefully.

"That's what I don't like," Andy said. "He's cute, and

I didn't mean to make a cute one. So now I'm going to build a bigger and better one, a real man who will work for me and be useful."

"Honestly?" Sparrow marveled. "Can you really do that?"

"I sure can," said Andy. The admiration and surprise in Sparrow's voice made him feel happy and boastful.

"Here's Grandpa," Sparrow said. "Grandpa, this is Andy

Buckram, a boy in my room at school. And look what he's built. It's a robot, Grandpa."

"Why, so it is," said Grandpa Clayton. "Does it work?"

"Yes, sir, it does," said Andy proudly.

Grandpa Clayton was a small old man with a little white beard like a snowball on the end of his chin. He had very twinkly blue eyes under bushy white brows. He stood in the doorway of his house, and Andy saw that the house, like everything else in the Automobile Graveyard and Spare Parts Lot, was made up of odd bits and leftover pieces.

Large flattened pieces of tin and old barn doors and packing crates and all sorts of unusual materials had gone into the construction of the house. Yet it had a delightful appearance of home and ease and good living. Old ladders had been erected across the front to form an arbor, upon which a grapevine grew, providing both shade from the sun and an abundance of fruit. Beneath the grapevine old automobile seats made pleasant benches.

"He needs to plug it in, Grandpa," Sparrow said. "It works by electricity."

"Well, come in. Let's see."

When his eyes became accustomed to the dimmer light, the inside of the house amazed Andy as much as the outside. The table had driftwood legs, and the dining chairs were made of old barrels. More automobile seats made sofas, and the cupboard was made of various-sized boxes neatly fitted together.

Grandpa Clayton turned on the lamp, and Andy saw

that it was made of an oddly shaped piece of driftwood and an automobile headlight. The shade was made of a very large tin can with top and bottom removed and the sides punched full of holes to let the light come through.

"Grandpa made it," Sparrow said. Andy looked at the old man with new respect. Here was an inventive person like himself.

"All right. Plug him in," said Grandpa Clayton, as he removed the lamp plug from the socket.

Andy unwound the cord from around Campbell's middle and plugged it into the socket. He set Campbell carefully on his feet and turned the "go" switch. Campbell's eyes lit up, he shivered all over, then he began to walk directly toward Sparrow.

"Oh, he limps!" cried Sparrow. "The darling thing!"

Campbell limped right over to Sparrow and tilted up his head as if he were looking at her and held up his arms to be taken.

"Oh, the cute, dear thing!" cried Sparrow. "He's only a *baby* robot!"

Andy was so ashamed of Campbell that he turned him off, and he could hardly bear to look at Grandpa Clayton to see what he would think. But Grandpa Clayton said heartily, "Why, that's excellent for a start. This is your first one, isn't it?"

"Yes," Andy said uncomfortably. "I meant him to be a man, but he turned out like this."

"Well, that's all right," Grandpa Clayton said. "It takes

33

all sorts of people to make a world, and I expect it's the same with robots. What do you plan for your next one?"

So then Andy began to describe Bucket to Grandpa Clayton, and they both got very interested and excited.

"Come out into the lot, Andy," Grandpa Clayton said. "We'll see what we can find."

"I don't have very much money left," Andy said. "That's one of my troubles."

"Money?" Grandpa Clayton said. "It's never been a trouble to *me*, Andy. I care so little about it that I'll be very happy to give you some good bargains. If a project interests me, I never ask how much money it will bring in."

"Still, I would like to pay what's fair," Andy said.

"Well, most of the things I have here," said Grandpa Clayton, "I got for nothing. People have thrown all this good stuff away. I have a kind of funny feeling that even old bits of tin and leather and wood like to be appreciated. I won't exactly say that they want to be loved. That's a little strong maybe. But, as long as there's any use in them, they want to be used. So I'm always glad when I can find a new life for some old thing that's been thrown away as lost and done for."

While they went from heap to heap, choosing cans and wires and chains and bolts, Sparrow trailed behind them, carrying Campbell. She felt more interested in the baby robot who was finished than in the man they planned to build.

Andy selected a small oil drum for a body and a kerosene

can for a head. Grandpa Clayton found an old battery that worked very well and would fit inside the oil drum.

"I wonder if some strong stovepipes wouldn't do for legs," he suggested.

"I'd like them to be jointed at the knees and hips," Andy said.

"Well, I'll tell you how to arrange that," Grandpa Clayton said, and he launched into a grave technical discussion which interested Andy very much. But Sparrow did not care how you made movable joints in stovepipe legs. She sat down on an overturned packing case and held Campbell as if he were a doll and moved his tin arms and legs.

"You're very cute," she said to him. "I hope Andy will bring you back again and let me play with you." It almost seemed to her that Campbell smiled at her.

When Andy rowed back up the river (after bailing out the boat, of course), he felt tired but very happy. Piled all around Campbell in the stern of the boat were the parts and pieces that would soon become Bucket, and they had not cost a penny. Grandpa Clayton claimed that they were all rubbish that careless people had thrown away, and he was glad to pass them on to Andy. So naturally Andy whistled and sang as he rowed. Although he did not stop to think what he whistled, it was of course "The Old Oaken Bucket." And now Andy could hardly wait to begin work on his second tin man.

Bucket

Bucket was harder to make than Campbell had been, but now Andy had much more experience, and he started right to work.

"Andy, you aren't going to make another one, are you?" wailed his mother.

"Just one more, Mama," Andy said. "You'll see. This one will be much more useful than Campbell. This one will do work."

"Ah," said Andy's father, "if he will do work, he will be a blessing around this place. Some boys I could mention, not a thousand miles away, don't do very much work these days."

36

"Daddy," Andy said, "I watered all the animals and cleaned the barn, and the chickens let themselves out because of my spring chicken roost, and I don't know what else I had to do."

"You could always calk and paint the boat, son."

"But Daddy, it only leaks a little, small amount, and there's lots of time before the rainy season sets in."

"All right," Mr. Buckram said, "but see that this robot really does some work to pay for all the time you put into making him."

Bucket turned out to be as tall as Andy himself, and to be very strong. Andy took care to paint a grown-up face on him, with mustache and a frown, so that he looked very serious. He had three controls. One made him lean over to fill his buckets; the second made him walk where directed, carrying them very carefully; the third made him tilt forward and dump the water into the trough.

Of course Andy had to go right along beside him and press the proper buttons at the proper time. He could not sit under a tree and pick his teeth while Bucket did his work for him. But at least Andy's arms would no longer ache from carrying heavy pails.

When Bucket was ready for his first trial, Mr. and Mrs. Buckram came out to watch.

"He'll never do it," Mr. Buckram said gloomily, and Mrs. Buckram said, "Oh, mercy! I hope not! And isn't he ugly?"

Andy felt nervous, as any inventor is likely to be at the

first trial of a new invention. He set Bucket up by the pump and pulled the switch which started the battery. Bucket's eyes lit up, and he began to make a businesslike humming sound.

"Oh, frogs and catfish!" cried Andy delightedly. He pressed the first control, and Bucket leaned forward and lowered his buckets so that Andy could fill them at the pump.

"Look at that!" marveled Mr. Buckram, and Mrs. Buckram cried, "My! My!"

When the buckets were full, Andy pressed the second control. Bucket straightened up with a whirring noise, turned around, and began to walk briskly across the barnyard.

Andy felt so excited that he could not help jumping up and down and shouting, "Hooray!"

"Oh, my darling boy!" cried Mrs. Buckram, folding Andy in her arms. "You are a genius, sure enough!"

"Congratulations, Andy," said Mr. Buckram. "I knew all the time it would be a success. Let me shake your hand."

While they were rejoicing, Bucket kept right on walking. The chickens ran squawking in every direction, and the pigs began to squeal. Old Daisy and the other cows began to bawl, and the horses to neigh and rear. Bucket walked right over to the pigpen fence and poured water all over the backs of the squealing, scurrying pigs. If Andy had not run fast and turned him off, Bucket would have walked through the fence and smack into the silo.

The barnyard was in an uproar. The animals were frightened out of their wits, and it took a long time to calm them.

"Well!" said Mr. Buckram. "If that's the way the new robot behaves, you had better break him up and throw him in the river." And Mrs. Buckram said, "Dear little Campbell. I love him best anyway."

But Andy did not give up hope.

"He only needs a little, small adjustment, Daddy," he said. "I should have watched him closer the first time, and not let him get away. I'm sure the animals will get used to him when they have seen him around for a while."

It took several days of adjustment and trial before Andy learned how to control the new robot. In the meantime, of course, he had to mend the pigpen fence and carry the water himself. But finally everything was in order.

With Andy beside him, Bucket would carry his pails carefully across the barnyard in whatever direction Andy headed him. At the proper instant Andy would turn the third control, and Bucket would empty his water into the right trough. Then the tin man would straighten himself, turn, and march back to the pump, with Andy close beside him.

Andy's parents were much impressed, but still Mr. Buckram sometimes grumbled that Andy worked harder making the robot behave properly than he would have if he carried the water himself.

"But Daddy, this is a lot more fun," Andy said, and, of course, that was true.

That first week the cows would not give down their milk nor the hens lay their eggs; and the veterinarian had to be called to give the pigs some pills to keep them from squealing. But presently the animals all got used to Bucket, as Andy had said they would, and the farm fell back into its old routine.

In fact, when Andy had taught Bucket to carry feed as well as water to the creatures, the chickens and cows grew very fond of the tin man. Chickens are curious and adaptable creatures, and soon they would fly up and ride along on Bucket's shoulders. The cows looked up with pleasure when they saw him coming, and old Daisy would even follow him about as if she loved him. Only the excitable pigs never did get used to him.

When Bucket was not working, Andy took him to his room and set him in the one chair where Andy's Levis used to be hung at night. Now he hung his Levis over the foot of the bed. Andy's room was small, and Bucket seemed to occupy a large part of it. But Andy loved to wake at night and see Bucket sitting there alert and watchful in the moonlight.

Andy even grew more fond of Campbell, now that he had made Bucket, and he was proud to see the smaller robot sitting in his smaller chair beside the big one. Andy felt happy, and he did not have any plans at this time for building another robot.

But he did feel that he ought to go down the river and show Bucket to the Claytons. They had been so helpful in creating the tin man that they would certainly like to see how he had turned out.

So one fine summer day, when he had finished his work, Andy bailed the boat and put Bucket in the stern seat and rowed and drifted down the river to the Automobile Graveyard and Spare Parts Lot.

"If I could make a robot who would row!" Andy thought as he went down the river. But then he remembered that he did not intend to make any more robots. Just as he had pushed off from shore, his mother had called, "Be home in time for dinner, Andy. And don't bring back any more junk, dear. You've done real well to make two robots. Now you ought to be satisfied."

"I am satisfied, Mama," Andy called back, "and I'll be home for dinner."

But was he satisfied? Andy did not feel sure about that. Making robots is something like eating peanuts. It does no good to say, "This is the last peanut," because you are sure to want just one more.

Sparrow Has an Idea

Sparrow Clayton had a couple of tubs set up on boxes beside the back door in preparation for her weekly washing. Sparrow was a good worker and an excellent housekeeper, but she did not enjoy washing. The rubbing and wringing and hanging out did not bother her, but pumping and lifting all that water made her back ache. So when she saw Andy Buckram's boat coming downriver she was glad of an excuse to postpone her washing until later.

She left the empty tubs sitting by the back door and ran down the path to the dock.

"Did you bring Campbell?" she called.

"No," said Andy, "I brought Bucket, the new one."

"Oh," said Sparrow with a note of disappointment in her voice. "Is that Bucket, sitting in the back?"

"Yes. Isn't he great?"

"He's big," said Sparrow.

"Taller than you are," said Andy proudly.

"He's ugly," said Sparrow.

"Well, he can't help that," said Andy. "I made him that way. I didn't want another cute robot on my hands. But wait until you see what he can do. Bucket is useful."

Sparrow did not say anything, but she stood at the land end of the dock, watching while Andy moored the boat. She could not make up her mind whether to like Bucket or not.

Andy carefully set the robot up on the river end of the dock and headed him toward the shore. He made the battery connection, and Bucket's eyes lit up. Sparrow heard a strange whirring noise that made her flesh creep. Then Andy pushed the number-two button, and Bucket began to walk briskly along the dock directly toward Sparrow.

At once Sparrow made up her mind that she did not like Bucket. She began to run up the bank toward her house, shouting, "Help! Help! He's after me! Help!"

"Why, Sparrow," Andy said, "he's only a tin man, for goodness' sake!"

But Sparrow continued to run and scream, with Bucket climbing briskly along after her. Andy was so charmed to see that the battery was strong enough to make Bucket climb uphill that he could not bear to stop him until he had reached the top.

"Oh, frogs and catfish!" he cried. "I never tried him on a hill before. He's marvelous! He's simply wonderful!"

Just in time, he turned Bucket off before the robot walked through the side of the Claytons' house. Sparrow had run inside and slammed the door. But when the robot stopped she opened the door a crack and peered out.

"I think he's horrible," she said.

"No, he isn't, Sparrow," Andy said. "He works much better than Campbell. Come out and see. I'll let you work him yourself."

"I'm afraid of him," Sparrow said.

"Don't be silly," said Andy. "The animals were all afraid of him, but they soon got used to him. I hope you have more sense than a pig or a chicken."

"I don't think I do," said Sparrow, opening the door a little wider.

"Listen," Andy said, "do you want these washtubs filled?"

"Yes. I was just going to do it when I saw your boat coming."

"All right," Andy said. "Now watch and see if you don't think Bucket is a useful robot."

Andy made Bucket walk to the pump and lean over to get his buckets filled. Then he made him straighten up and walk to the tubs and pour the water into them.

Sparrow opened the door quite wide and stood there watching. It was very interesting to see her tubs being filled so easily and efficiently.

"Mercy me!" she said.

45

Grandpa Clayton had been out in the Automobile Grave-yard when he heard Sparrow's screams, and now he came up in time to see Bucket filling the washtubs.

"Well, well, well!" he said. He and Sparrow stood together, watching.

Andy showed them how to work the switches, and each one took a turn at making Bucket pour water into the tubs.

"Now you aren't scared any more, are you, Sparrow?" Andy asked.

"No-o-o," said Sparrow. "I respect him, but I don't think I'd ever love him."

"Nobody asked you to love him," Andy said. "He's a tin man, for goodness' sake!"

"Well, it's a mechanical age," Grandpa Clayton said. "Soon everything will be done for us by tin men, I expect. You are very smart, my boy, to be in on the ground floor, so to speak. What kind of robot do you plan to build next?"

"I'm not planning on building any more," Andy said. "I've got to calk and paint the boat the next thing I do."

"I see," Grandpa Clayton said. "Does the boat leak very badly?"

"Not badly yet," Andy said, "but Daddy wants it done before the rainy season starts. After the fall rains come, it's hard to get the bottom of the boat dry enough to make the paint stick on."

"True enough," Grandpa Clayton said. "Your father is quite right. Still, the rainy season is a long way off yet,

and you like to use the boat during the summer. I expect you would have to turn it upside down out on shore for several days before it gets dry enough to calk and paint, wouldn't you? That would mean that you couldn't use it for at least a week, wouldn't it?"

"Yes," Andy said, "and, of course, Cousin Eva might

want me to baby-sit with her Dot during that time, and I wouldn't have the boat to row up the river. I expect Daddy didn't think about that."

"Well, you must always do what your Daddy and Mother tell you to do, Andy."

"I try to," Andy said, "but there really doesn't seem to be much need to hurry with the boat."

"Andy," Sparrow said. Her eyes were bright with excitement. "I've been thinking. Why don't you make a girl robot?"

"A *girl?*" repeated Andy. "What would that be good for?"

"Well!" Sparrow said in a huff. "Girls are good for a lot of things that boys aren't good for."

Andy was about to say, "Name one," when Grandpa Clayton said, "Now, Sparrow, I expect Andy's mother has told him not to bring home any more junk. She probably thinks that two robots are enough for any boy."

"Why, how did you know, sir?" asked Andy in surprise.

"I just guessed," Grandpa Clayton said. "It's a normal reaction, and I'm sure that she is right."

"But I don't think that she would really mind very much," Andy said, "just so I get home in time for dinner."

"And I have another idea, Andy," Sparrow said. "I wish you would make a robot that could talk or sing."

"Well, I've thought about that," Andy said. "But I don't know any way, unless I put a little record player inside."

"Grandpa's got some parts of an old record changer and player in his tool shed, haven't you, Grandpa?"

"Yes," Grandpa Clayton said thoughtfully, "but they would be heavy. The robot would have to be fat in the body and sturdy in the legs."

"I could plug her in like Campbell," said Andy, "and then she wouldn't have to carry a battery as well as a record player. That would help some."

"Still, she would have to be fat and sturdy," Grandpa Clayton said.

"Um-m-m," murmured Andy dreamily. He thought very hard, and he began to feel excited. "A girl robot," he said to himself, "a fat girl who could talk and sing. I could call her Lily Belle. I don't know what she would be good for, but I'd like to try it. Do you have a good, sturdy oil drum, Mr. Clayton, that would hold a record player?"

"We can look, son," Grandpa Clayton said. And so they went right out to look.

Andy got home in time for dinner that night, but all around Bucket in the back of the boat were the parts and pieces that would make Lily Belle.

Andy felt so pleased and excited with his new project that he even forgot how hard it was to row upriver in a leaky boat. "A fat girl robot who can talk and sing," he kept saying to himself, and his head was full of plans. Without really knowing what he was doing, he began to hum and sing,

"Ring, ring, lily bells ring, the blossoms are coming to town."

49

Lily Belle was taller than Campbell and shorter than Bucket. She could move her arms and walk if necessary, but she had a heavy body, and she preferred to sit still and talk or sing. Her short, sturdy legs were made of large tomato-juice cans with slightly smaller grapefruit-juice cans fitted inside them for extra strength.

Inside her oil-drum body, Andy assembled the parts of the record player. It was a good-sized record player, and there had to be lots of little wheels and gadgets to make it play, as well as pulleys and drive shafts to make the robot's other parts move. After all this equipment was inside Lily Belle's body, there was not much room for records. Even ten-inch records were awkward to use. Andy had to make several trips back to the Graveyard and Spare Parts Lot before he had everything he needed.

But Grandpa Clayton finally discovered three old-time six-inch records among his spare parts. These were still in good condition and they would fit Lily Belle nicely.

"You're welcome to them, Andy," he said. "I am not sure how suitable they are, but they will give you variety at least. They are not long-playing records. Each one will play only a short time, but that's really a good thing. Lily Belle need never be a bore by going on too long with the same tune."

Andy took the records with thanks. The fact that they would fit Lily Belle's body interested him more than how they would sound.

Only Sparrow read the titles and seemed interested in what Lily Belle would say or sing.

"'Rockabye, Baby, on the Treetop,'" she read on the first record, "'sung by soprano voice.' Well, that's all right. Campbell will enjoy hearing that, and I think it's quite suitable. But I don't know about this one. It's called 'The Merry Yodeler's Dream.'"

"Oh, that will be fine," said Andy. "I love yodeling."

"And this one," Sparrow said, "it doesn't sound suitable at all."

"What is it?"

"It's a speech by Senator Quackenbush, whoever that

51

is," said Sparrow. "It doesn't sound like my idea of a girl robot at all."

"But these are the only records of the proper size that your Grandpa could find," Andy said. "I'm sure it will be all right."

"And another thing, Andy," Sparrow said. "I don't think that Lily Belle *looks* like a girl. If she has all kinds of voices and looks like any other robot, what's the use of calling her a girl?"

Andy thought about this. After all, Lily Belle was Sparrow's idea, and he wanted to please Sparrow because she had been so helpful to him in other ways.

"I'll tell you what," he said. "Instead of tiny flashlight bulbs, I'll give Lily Belle blue Christmas-tree-bulb eyes. And I'll make her a lot of tin curls. You know the tin strips that you unwind from coffee cans with a little key? Well, after the strip is wound on the key, if you hold the outside of the strip and pull the key downwards, you can make very good curls. I used to make Christmas-tree decorations that way. I'll make her a whole lot of tin curls, Sparrow, and solder them on. Will that please you?"

"Ye-e-s," Sparrow said, "that should help, and I'll give you a blue hair ribbon and an old blue apron to tie around her middle. Still, I really don't know about the Senator's speech, Andy. That seems very strange."

"But if we don't use that we'll have only two records, Sparrow," Andy said, "and they're both so short. I really think we need three. Who cares if they're not all in the same voice. She's only a tin man—I mean girl—anyway."

"All right," Sparrow said. "Try it and see."

Lily Belle's head was made of two small tin basins soldered together. Andy painted a sweet smile on her face, and he took a hammer and chisel and pounded a dimple into each cheek. He made ten beautiful curls and soldered them all around the back of her head. It was the first time that he had bothered to make a robot look like something. The fact that Campbell looked like a baby had been accidental, and Andy had made Bucket look grim simply because he did not want him to turn out to be another baby. But, because of Sparrow, Andy tried hard to make a beauty of Lily Belle. He was fairly well pleased with the result.

When he plugged her in and turned the first switch, her blue bulb eyes gleamed. She began to make a gentle purring noise, then a flip-flop sound, and, almost at once, she began to sing in a very sweet voice.

> "Rockabye, baby, on the treetop,
>   When the wind blows
>   The cradle will rock.
>   When the bough breaks
>   The cradle will fall,
>   And down will come rockabye
>   Baby, and all."

Andy's mother was delighted. "However did you give her such a sweet voice, son?" she cried. She had almost forgotten that this was only a record.

Mr. Buckram said, "Well, my boy, you've done it again! You're quite a genius."

Lily Belle sat in the best chair and sang several more nursery rhymes. Then the record stopped, there was a little pause, followed by a purring noise and a flip-flopping sound, and then the second record started.

"The Merry Yodeler's Dream" turned out to be a very jolly record, full of laughing "ha-ha-ha"s and "ho-ho-ho"s followed by many "yo-lally-yo-lally"s. The whole effect was so merry that Andy and his father and his mother all began to laugh too. The house fairly rocked with their laughter.

"Wait until Sparrow hears this!" cried Andy, wiping his eyes. "This is really good."

Silence, whirr, flip-flop. Then suddenly a great booming voice began to speak.

"My friends," roared Lily Belle in Senator Quackenbush's voice, "now is the time to awaken to the dangers which surround us. The situation is very grave. Something must be done immediately. In these trying times we ask your help and confidence. We ask—"

Andy turned Lily Belle off in the middle of the Senator's speech because the telephone was ringing. But he was pleased with his work. What if the speech did not sound like a girl robot? It was very impressive, just the same, and Andy felt proud of himself for creating a robot who could make a political speech. He liked it better than the "Rocka-bye, Baby" bit.

"Andy," Mrs. Buckram said as she came back from the telephone, "Cousin Eva wants to know, can you sit with Dot tonight? There's a new movie at the Bijou Theatre, and Eva and Samuel would like to go."

"All right, Mama," Andy said. "I'll go if I can take Lily Belle."

"Well, why not, son?" said Andy's mother. "Dot might be quite amused." She went back to the telephone. "Yes, Eva," she said, "he'll be very pleased to come."

So, late in the afternoon, Andy put Lily Belle in the stern of the boat, and, after bailing for some time, he began to row up the river.

"If this works, as I hope it will," Andy said to himself, "it will really be quite an invention."

He carried Lily Belle up from the dock and sat her down in one of Cousin Eva's kitchen chairs near the electric outlet where Cousin Eva usually plugged in her toaster.

"What in the world is that?" asked Cousin Eva. Dot just stared at Lily Belle with wide blue eyes and forgot to bang her heels and yell. Lily Belle stared back at Dot, her unlighted bulb eyes as blue and round as Dot's.

"It's my newest robot," Andy said. "I've made three now, and I think I'll make one more, if I can figure how to invent a robot that will row a boat."

"A *what?*" asked Cousin Eva.

"A robot," Andy said patiently, "a tin man, you know. Only this is a tin girl. She sings, and I thought that Dot might like her."

"She doesn't have any loose parts that Dot could accidentally swallow, does she?"

"Oh, no, she's well soldered."

"Then that's all right," Cousin Eva said. "And, of course, you know about not letting Dot have her cooky until she has eaten her soup, and about her pink pajamas with the bunnies on them?"

"Yes, I know," Andy said.

When Dot saw that her mother and father were going to the movies, leaving her alone with Andy, she forgot to stare at the robot and she began to scream and bang her heels.

"She'll be all right in a moment, Andy," said Cousin Eva as she went out the door. "I know she'll be a real good girl."

Andy was not so sure, but he felt more hopeful than he had ever felt before. He carefully moved the grape jelly out of Dot's reach and began to heat the soup. Then he went around to the back of Lily Belle's chair and plugged her cord into the toaster socket. He snapped the first control switch, and Lily Belle's large blue eyes flashed on. She began to make a pleasant purring noise, then there was a flip-flop sound and she started to laugh.

"Ha-ha-ha-ha-ha! Ho-ho-ho-ho-ho!" laughed Lily Belle. "Yo-lally-yo-lally-yo-lally."

Dot had been screaming and banging, but now she stopped as if someone had switched her off. She sat perfectly still, listening and looking at Lily Belle with great

astonishment. Andy scarcely dared to breathe. Would Dot be frightened and go off into worse fits of howling? Or would she settle down and be entertained? He did not know what to expect.

But the miracle happened, and Dot decided to be entertained. In a moment she was laughing as hard as Lily Belle.

"Ha-ha-ha-ha-ha!" laughed Dot. "Ho-ho-ho-ho-ho!" Before the record ended she even began shouting, "Lally-yo! Lally-yo!"

Andy managed to get quite a few spoonfuls of soup into Dot between "ha"s and "ho"s and "lally-yo"s.

Then there came a pause, a purr, and a flip-flop.

"Eat now, baby," urged Andy, feeding Dot another spoonful of soup. "Eat it up." He was worried about Dot's reaction to Senator Quackenbush, and he wanted to get as much food into her as possible before she began to scream again.

"My friends," roared Lily Belle, "now is the time to awaken to the dangers which surround us. The situation is very grave." Dot stopped eating. Her lower lip began to droop in a threatening manner. She gave a kick with her heels on the step of the high chair. Her eyes closed, and her face began to pucker for a terrible wail.

"Listen, baby, it's a nice, nice man. A daddy-man," said Andy in a soothing voice.

"Daddy?" asked Dot, opening her eyes and unpuckering her face.

"A nice, nice man," repeated Andy.

"No-no-no," said Dot, puckering up again. "I-da-wa-nim! I-da-wa-nim! No-no-no!" She really began to howl then, the worst Andy had ever heard.

But at that moment something strange happened to the noise that was coming out of Lily Belle. She had just arrived at the part of the record which said, "We ask your help and confidence."

"We ask your help! help! help! help—" roared Lily Belle.

For an instant Andy was fooled into thinking that Lily

Belle really needed help. Between howling Dot and roaring Lily Belle, he did not know what to do next.

But when Dot heard Lily Belle screaming for help, she suddenly turned pleasant again and began to eat her soup. For a baby Dot had an odd sense of humor, and now she laughed pleasantly between mouthfuls of soup.

"Poor baby!" she said, pointing a dripping spoon at Lily Belle and laughing happily.

"Help! help! help!" roared Lily Belle.

Dot had finished her soup and started on her first cooky before Andy discovered what was wrong with Lily Belle. Apparently, as he had moved her about from place to place, the Senator's record had become slightly cracked. The needle stuck at "help" and would not go any farther. Finally Andy slapped Lily Belle on the back, as he would have slapped the baby if she had choked on a piece of cooky. Lily Belle gave a little gasp and then went on calmly, "and confidence. We ask your patience and under-standing."

By the time Lily Belle had finished her speech and flip-flopped to "Rockabye, Baby," Dot was on her ninth cooky, and her eyes looked very sleepy.

"Down," she said. Andy lifted her out of her high chair, and she began to toddle toward the robot.

"Baby, don't touch," said Andy. "Here's your b'anky."

Dot took her old shred of blanket and pressed it to her cheek. Before Andy could stop her, she climbed into Lily Belle's lap and laid her head on the robot's tin shoulder.

" 'When the bough breaks, the cradle will fall,' " sang Lily Belle sweetly. Dot put her thumb in her mouth, gave a long, contented sigh, and went to sleep.

When he was sure that Dot was sound asleep for the night, Andy turned Lily Belle off and carried Dot very carefully to her crib. She had a lovely smile on her face, and she really did look like a nice child when she was asleep.

Andy said softly to himself, "And I thought that Lily Belle was not going to be useful! She's worth her weight in gold."

Supercan

Andy planned the fourth robot on magnificent lines. This tin man was six feet tall, and he had every improvement that Andy could possibly devise. Andy planned him first of all so that he would sit in the boat and row. But by this time he had become so experienced as a robot builder that he kept thinking of new things for the man to do. He certainly wanted him to row, but he also thought that it would be good if the robot could use his head as well as his arms. For instance, if he could do sums while rowing upstream and subtract while rowing down—wouldn't that be something?

Andy had to make a lot of trips to Grandpa Clayton's

before he found everything he needed. The arithmetic part, of course, caused the most difficulty until Grandpa Clayton found a small computer. It had been thrown away because a later model had taken its place. But Andy thought that by attaching a little bell to the computer he might make the new robot do his figuring for him.

"What are you going to call the new tin man, Andy?" asked Sparrow.

"I thought about Rowbot," Andy said. "How do you like that?"

"But that's what he is, a robot."

"But I would spell it R-O-W-B-O-T, or B-O-A-T, if you like that better."

"I don't care how you spell it," objected Sparrow, "it doesn't sound grand enough for this tin man. He's really going to be super."

"Super," mused Andy. "Superman, Supercan—"

"Supercan!" cried Sparrow. "That's it! That's a perfectly lovely name. And you can trim him up with knobs and handles and watchchains and doodads! He'll be the fanciest tin man anyone ever made."

"Supercan," said Andy. "Yes, I think that's good. I'll call him Supercan."

The wiring was difficult, but finally Andy got the computer rigged up and attached to a little bell inside Supercan. When Andy wanted to add two and two, he pressed certain buttons on Supercan's back. There was a whirring and clattering and then the little bell rang four times. Of course anyone can add two and two. But say Andy wanted to multiply five by six. He pressed the right buttons and listened to the whirr and clatter, and then the bell would ring thirty times.

Mr. Buckram said, "The only trouble is, Andy, that by the time you have counted the thirty strokes of the bell you might as well have figured out the arithmetic in your own head or on your own fingers."

"But that wouldn't be so much fun," Andy said, and, of course, this was true.

Andy had become so interested in the computer that he had gone ahead working on that before he ever tried Supercan out in the boat on the river. But one fine day he carefully bailed the boat and got it ready. Then he set Supercan on his feet by the back door and started him walking down to the river. It was impossible to carry him, because he had a large battery as well as the computer inside him, and he was heavy.

Mr. and Mrs. Buckram went along, and several neighbors who had heard about Andy's robots arrived in time to watch.

The farm animals were now used to Bucket, and, because he brought them food and water, they were becoming fond of him. But when they saw Supercan striding down the hill they all went wild again. The horses raced and whinnied, the cows bawled and kicked their legs in the air, the chickens flopped and squawked. Even after taking the pills which the veterinarian had left for them, the pigs squealed and ran, and all the curl came out of their tails.

"I don't know," Mr. Buckram said. "It doesn't seem like this sort of thing should be done on a farm—in a factory, maybe, but not on a farm."

"Daddy," Andy said, "they'll get used to Supercan, just the way they got used to Bucket."

Andy naturally felt nervous, as he always did on a first trial of one of his robots. Yet he believed that nothing could possibly go wrong with Supercan, who was surely his masterpiece.

When they reached the river, Andy switched off the walking control. Supercan stood quietly, waiting for the next command. He was a magnificent sight with the sun shining on his vast expanse of dazzling tin.

"Wonderful!" the neighbors said.

Now Andy rolled up his Levis so that he could wade in the river beside the boat while he hoisted Supercan into it. This was quite a job, but Andy managed to lift and push the robot into the boat, and then he carefully arranged him on the rower's seat. Andy had built Supercan's hands so that they would clamp tightly about the oars, and now he put an oar into each of the tin man's hands. Next Andy pushed the boat out into the water and turned on Supercan's motor. Andy had intended to get into the boat to control the robot, but, before he had time to jump aboard, Supercan began to row. It all happened very quickly.

The boat shot out from shore into the river. Supercan

bobbed up and down, up and down, and at every bob the little bell rang. The oars flashed in and out of the water at a terrible rate of speed.

"Oh, he's going away, Andy!" cried Mrs. Buckram, and Mr. Buckram said, "Andy, my boy, you're losing your tin man—and after all that work, too!"

Andy did not have to be told that he was losing his tin man. He gave a cry of despair as he saw his masterpiece rowing rapidly out into deep water.

"As soon as the current gets him, he will be a goner, Andy," cried the neighbors cheerfully.

But when the boat reached midstream a curious thing happened. Instead of rowing away, up or down the river, Supercan began rowing around and around in circles in the middle of the river. There he was, bobbing furiously up and down, while the oars flashed in and out of the water and the bell tinkled. But the boat just kept going around in large circles in front of the Buckrams' landing.

"Well, son, what are you going to do?" asked Mr. Buckram. Everybody looked at Andy, and Andy scratched his head. The only thing he could think to do was to swim out to the boat and try to catch hold of it as it flashed by. So that is what he did. Andy swam well, but it was hard to catch up with the boat at the rate Supercan was rowing. In the midst of his troubles, however, Andy could not help thinking that he had really succeeded in creating a mighty fine rower.

Finally Andy decided to swim to a spot on the circle

which the boat was making and to wait there until the boat came by. Then he managed to catch hold of *Dorinda's* stern and hang on. Presently he was able to climb aboard, tumbling over the side and into the bottom of the boat at Supercan's feet. After that it took Andy only a moment to turn the robot off and row the boat back to shore himself.

"Too bad!" everybody said, and Mr. Buckram said, "Think of the hours you wasted, Andy, working on this hunk of tin."

But Andy said, "Daddy, all he needs is a little, small adjustment. The trouble is that one arm works a little harder than the other. He pulls harder on the right oar than on the left one, and that is what makes the boat go around in circles. But it's lucky he worked that way this first time, or I really would have lost him. Next time I'll get into the boat with him before I turn him on."

Of course Andy was right, and before long he had Supercan working perfectly. Now, when Andy wished to go up- or downriver, he could sit at ease in the seat behind Supercan and make the robot do all the rowing. When Andy wanted to fish, he simply turned Supercan off, dropped the anchor beside a nice quiet hole, preferably in the shade, fished as long as he liked, and later turned Supercan on again to row home. Of course Andy still had to bail the boat, but he was used to that.

Sometimes, if the fish were not biting well, Andy amused himself by turning on the robot's calculating machine. The little bell could be heard up and down the river, busily solving Andy's arithmetic problems. Supercan could figure up to ten times ten. But Andy found that by the time he had counted one hundred tinkles of the bell he was quite worn out and had probably missed a few tinkles here and there along the way.

However, Supercan made Andy more famous in the neighborhood than he had ever been. People from all up and down the river began to come to the Buckrams' farm to see Andy's robots. Naturally so much favorable attention pleased Andy, but his parents complained that it was difficult to get their work done with so many visitors popping in. But they were proud of Andy just the same. Even Sparrow and Grandpa Clayton promised to come up one day to see all Andy's robots working together.

Still Andy had one difficulty in his home life at this time. Now that he had four robots, his bedroom was really a mess.

Lily Belle, because she was a lady and a bit too fat, naturally occupied the chair at the foot of the bed where Andy's Levis used to hang at night. Campbell sat beside her in the baby chair. But where to put the other two robots?

Andy found that there was just enough room for Bucket to stand between the chest of drawers and the wall. But whenever Andy opened a drawer to get out a clean shirt he crashed into a bucket, and it became rather awkward.

At first there seemed to be no place at all for Supercan. But finally Andy crammed the largest tin man into his closet, along with his Sunday clothes, his hammers and tools, his fishing rods and tackle, his Scrabble game, the violin case that had belonged to Uncle Sam Buckram, and the piles of back numbers of *The Boy's Popular Mechanics Magazine* with which Andy could not bear to part. The closet was small, and all these things made a very tight fit. Sometimes, when Andy opened the closet door, everything fell out, including Supercan, and it was quite a job to get everything crammed back in.

Andy himself could have tolerated these small inconveniences. But his mother soon began to fret.

"Clyde," she said to Andy's father, "I know we have a genius for a son and all that, but really you ought to take a look at his room. It's just impossible. I can't sweep or dust or put away his clean clothes because of all these robots. You must speak to him."

"Hello, Andy," Mr. Buckram said. But that did not satisfy Mrs. Buckram at all.

"No, Clyde, I mean *really* speak to him. Tell him he's got to clear these robots out and put them some place else. The last time I opened his closet the big tin man fell right out and nearly knocked me over. It's come to a point where it's either me or the tin men in this house. Andy will have to choose. And I notice he hasn't yet invented a robot that can cook."

"Why, Mama," Andy said, for he stood right there and had heard every word, "I would rather have *you* than the robots, of course, but I don't know where else to keep them. The tool shed is full, and the granary is full, and you know the cows and horses would go crazy if I put the robots in the barn. The pigpen and the chicken house are out of the question for the same reason. But Mama, if you really want a robot that can cook, I'll begin to think about it—"

"No, no, son," said Mr. Buckram hastily. "Don't think about any more robots just now, for goodness' sake! We've got to take one problem at a time, and the present problem is what to do with the robots you have. Your mother must be able to clean your room without being knocked on the head by falling cans."

"I could always do without having my room cleaned, Mama," Andy said hopefully. But this idea did not appeal to Mrs. Buckram in the least. "Or we could get a tent and I could camp out."

"No, indeed," said Mrs. Buckram positively, "not while we have a house to live in."

"I'll tell you what, Andy," Mr. Buckram said. "There's that old turkey shed near the top of the hill under the big pine tree. It has been empty for years, and I don't see why you shouldn't keep your robots there."

"But there aren't any electrical outlets in it, Daddy."

"That's all right," Mr. Buckram said. "It's a fine storage place, and soon you are going to be calking and painting the boat, and then going to school. You won't have time to play with your tin men. All you really need is a high and dry place to store them for the winter."

"Very well, Daddy," Andy said. "But can I just wait a couple more days until Sparrow and Grandpa Clayton come over? I've promised to make all the robots work at once for them. After that I'll put them in the turkey shed."

"Fair enough," said Mr. Buckram, and Mrs. Buckram said, "I'll put off housecleaning your room for a few more days, Andy, until after I've made my apple butter."

So Andy had these few more days to enjoy the company of his robots.

Four at Once

Mrs. Buckram was making bread in the oven and cooking apple butter on the back of the electric stove on the day the Claytons came to call. It was the first cloudy day they had had all summer, and she turned the electric light on so that she could see to measure her sugar and spices. Andy had been helping his mother peel apples.

When they heard Grandpa Clayton's wagon come rattling into the yard, Mrs. Buckram said, "Go out and entertain them, Andy. I've got to change into a clean apron. First you can take Sparrow for a row on the river with Supercan, to show her how he works. Then bring them all in—Supercan too—and you can operate the robots all at once here in the kitchen, where I can see too."

"Fine, Mama," Andy said.

"And I'll give you milk and fresh bread and apple butter after the demonstration is over."

"Gee, Mama, thanks a lot," cried Andy.

Grandpa Clayton and Andy's father were already shaking hands in the yard, and Sparrow stood looking around as if she missed somebody.

"Here I am," said Andy.

"Hi," said Sparrow. "Where's Campbell?"

"I thought you were looking for *me*," said Andy.

"Well, you too," said Sparrow. "But I haven't seen Campbell for a long time, and he's so cute."

"You'll see him all right," Andy said. "But first I'll take you for a ride in the boat to show you how Supercan can row."

As they went down the path to the river Andy heard Grandpa Clayton saying, "You have a very clever and inventive boy here, Mr. Buckram."

"Yes, we're proud of Andy," Mr. Buckram replied. "Still, it's time now that he settled down to something useful like calking and painting the boat."

"I expect you are right," Grandpa Clayton said. "Summer is nearly over. The rainy season will soon be starting, and school will be starting too."

Andy and Sparrow hated to think that the eventful summer could ever end. Now they raced away to the river, and Andy set Supercan to rowing the boat. The tin man rowed them up and down the river and at the same time did Sparrow's sums for her.

"He's certainly a wonderful invention," Sparrow said.

"He sure is. Don't you think he's the best of the lot, Sparrow?"

"Well, he's very, very good, Andy, and I certainly enjoy riding around like this. But I still think that Lily Belle is the smartest, and I love the baby best."

"Baby!" scoffed Andy. "If you mean Campbell, you know he's really the oldest, though he's undersized and not very bright."

"I don't care," Sparrow said. "He's cute, and I love him."

When they came in from the river, with Supercan walking between them up the hill, they found the grownups already in the kitchen, waiting for the demonstration. Mrs. Buckram had on a clean apron, and the bread was out of the oven, but the apple butter was still bubbling on the back of the stove. The kitchen was full of delightful odors, and Sparrow lifted her nose and said, "Umm! Umm!"

But Andy was too eager to show off his robots to stop and sniff. Even knowing exactly what each robot would do, Andy still felt a trifle nervous, because he had never before operated them all at once. This would require some skill.

First he brought the other three robots out of his bedroom and arranged them in the kitchen. He set Lily Belle and Campbell near the electric outlets where Mrs. Buckram usually plugged in the toaster and the coffeepot. Campbell seemed to be smiling very specially at Sparrow and Mrs. Buckram, and Andy thought with disgust that, even when turned off, he still acted like a baby. Lily Belle, with her blue eyes and tin curls and blue hair ribbon and apron, looked like a good little fat girl ready to speak a piece on the last day of school.

With his mother's permission Andy seated Supercan on the edge of the kitchen table and clamped a broom handle in one of his hands and a mop handle in the other. Here he could show his rowing ability as well as in the boat, and, thank goodness, the table did not need bailing! Andy left Bucket standing in the middle of the kitchen floor, and he meant to head him out toward the pump as soon as everyone was turned on and operating.

First Andy started the two battery-operated robots. Supercan lighted up with a whirr and a jangle of his little bell. He began to work the broom and the mop as if they were oars. Bucket began to walk across the kitchen, while Andy rushed to plug in Campbell and Lily Belle. Lily Belle began to sing, and Campbell began to nod his head and hold up his arms.

Now Andy rushed to press the computer buttons on Supercan's back. "Four times four," he pressed, and Supercan's little bell began to jangle out sixteen strokes.

"Isn't it wonderful?" Mrs. Buckram cried. Above the noise of singing and ringing and whirring and purring, the

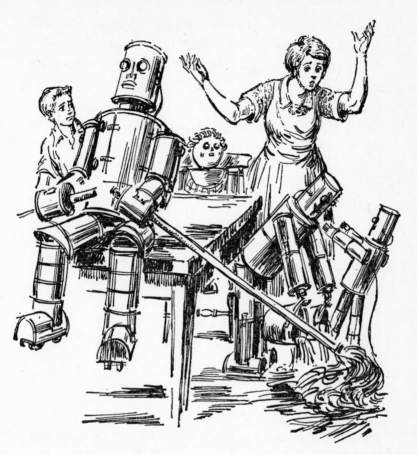

others shouted, "Perfectly wonderful! Who would have believed it possible?"

But while Andy busied himself with the computer controls nobody had been watching Bucket. He walked to the stove, dipped his bucket into the hot apple butter, turned around and dumped it onto the floor. Still ringing and rowing furiously, Supercan spread the hot apple butter all over the linoleum with his mop and his broom.

At the same time, what with the light, the stove, and the two smaller robots all going at once, the electrical circuit became overheated and a fuse blew out. The light went out, the stove went off, and Campbell and Lily Belle sat quietly in their chairs. But unfortunately Bucket and Supercan went right on doing what they were doing until Andy could switch them off.

For a moment he thought that Lily Belle was still operating, because someone certainly shouted, "Help! Help! Help!" But it turned out to be Andy's mother, who was quite disturbed about her apple butter and her clean floor and the fact that the electricity had gone off. "Help! Help! Help!" she cried.

The confusion was pretty bad for a while. For the first time it occurred to Andy to wonder if robots were worth all the effort it took to build them and keep them operating and out of trouble. It would have been easier to go camping, or even to calk and paint the boat. But as soon as he had thought this thought, Andy felt ashamed of himself. Here were all these four tin people looking at him with their light-bulb eyes, and he knew that he loved every one of them—even Campbell. Perhaps he would not build any more robots, but at least he would take care of these and try to keep them out of mischief.

"I'm sorry about this, Mama," Andy said. "They got a little, small bit out of control. That's all."

"Oh, my clean kitchen floor!" wailed Mrs. Buckram.

"I'll help Andy, Mrs. Buckram," Sparrow said. "We'll clean your kitchen like new."

"But what about my apple butter?"

"Mama, we'll pick you some more apples," Andy said.

"Well, son," said Mr. Buckram, "I guess you'd better not try to operate them all at once any more. I'll put a new fuse in the fuse box. But I declare to goodness, I've had enough of robots to last me the rest of my life. Pigs in the parlor are nothing compared to robots in the kitchen."

"Or in the bedroom either," Andy's mother said.

"It's a pity," said Grandpa Clayton. "I never saw a finer sight in my life than I saw that first minute, when all the robots were working together. But I can understand your parents' point of view, Andy. Enough is enough."

So that very afternoon Andy moved the tin people up the hill to the old turkey shed under the tall pine tree. First he and Sparrow cleaned up the mess in the kitchen, and then they carried or walked the robots up the steep bank and stored them away.

"Now, men—excuse me, Lily Belle—and ladies. Ladies and gentlemen," Andy said to the robots, "I hate to leave you way up here so far from my room. I'll really miss you. But I'll come up here every chance I get, and whenever Daddy will let me I'll put you to work down below. Good-by for now."

The robots looked at him sadly with their bulb eyes.

"Good-by for now. Good-by," Sparrow said softly, and

she threw a kiss to Campbell. "Oh, Andy, it was so wonderful when they were all working together at the same time. If we could only have them doing that right along, and still keep it under control!"

"I know," said Andy, "that's what I wish too. But I guess we have to be reasonable. Thank you for coming and helping, Sparrow." They both felt sad, and very soon Sparrow and her grandpa drove away.

Early the next morning Andy and his father pulled the boat up on shore and turned it upside down so that the water would drain out and the bottom get dry.

"Now we'll carry it halfway up the hill behind the house into that bare spot where the sun and air can get at it," Mr. Buckram said. "We'll put it across two sawhorses, bottom side up. When it's nice and dry you can begin to scrape the old paint off it. Next time I'm in town I'll get some putty and some white lead and some waterproof paint. What color would you like, Andy?"

Andy scratched his head and thought. He tried very hard to get up some enthusiasm for painting the boat. But today he felt as bleak as the dark, gray sky overhead.

"Really I don't care, Daddy," he said. "You pick out any color you want, and I'll put it on."

"Fine, Andy," Mr. Buckram said. "You're a good boy."

Lightning

With the robots put away and the boat drying out, Andy hoped to find some time for reading the back numbers of *The Boy's Popular Mechanics Magazine.*

But Mr. Buckram thought of a number of things about the farm that needed attention the very first morning.

"After you milk old Daisy, Andy, the cattle stalls need a good cleaning. Next a corner of the pigsty needs mending. After that you can start splitting some kindling for the parlor stove. It will soon be cold enough to light a fire in there. You have had your fun with robots this summer. Now it's time you did something useful."

"Daddy, we never got around to go camping, did we?"

79

"No, we didn't," Mr. Buckram said regretfully.

So Andy worked very hard all morning. As he cleaned up after the cows and mended the pigsty, he could not help thinking that it would be nice to have robot pigs and cows. Robots were so much cleaner than cows and pigs, and they did not need to be fed. But then, of course, they would not give milk nor turn into bacon or pork chops. Since working made Andy very hungry, he decided not to build any robot animals. At least not at the present time.

As Mrs. Buckram was calling her son and husband in for lunch, there came a sudden clap of thunder, and almost at once the rain began to fall. Andy and his father ran for the house, but they were drenched before they reached the warm, dry kitchen.

"Daddy, I'm afraid the boat won't dry out," Andy said. He sounded almost as sad as if he were really sorry.

"It is early for the rainy season," Mr. Buckram said. "This is only a shower. Tomorrow the sun will be shining, and the boat will dry out nicely."

But it rained all afternoon, and Andy had plenty of time to read his magazines. He lay on his bed and heard the rain beating on the roof, and he thought about his robots up the hill in the turkey shed. His room was very clean, and he could open his closet door and the drawers of his dresser without hitting anything or turning loose an avalanche of falling objects. The baby chair had gone back to the wood-shed, and he could hang his Levis on the big chair at the foot of the bed once more. Everything was beautifully neat and commodious. But Andy felt lonesome and a little sad.

In spite of Mr. Buckram's cheerful predictions, the sun did not shine the next day. The rain continued to fall. It seemed that the rainy season had set in early that year, taking everybody by surprise. For a week it rained and rained. Sometimes it would clear up for a short time, and the sun would come briefly out of the clouds. Then Andy would go up to look at the boat and test it with his finger to see how wet it was. It was always very wet. It steamed in the watery sunshine. Andy knew that any paint he might put on now would peel right off without doing any good. This went on for so long that Andy even began to think that it might be more fun to paint the boat than to stay indoors all day, reading *The Boy's Popular Mechanics Magazine*.

It would have been a wonderful time to build another robot, but Andy had used up all his spare parts, and it was too wet to go to Grandpa Clayton's Automobile Graveyard for more. Besides, the boat was high, if not dry, and it was senseless to lug it back to the river until it was properly repaired.

Sometimes Andy put on his raincoat and boots and climbed through the rain to the turkey shed to see his tin men. Since there was no electrical outlet in the shed, he could not do anything with Lily Belle or Campbell. Their cords were useless without a proper connection.

At first Andy worked Bucket and Supercan. He had put the oars and a steering paddle into the shed for safe keeping while the boat was out of use. By seating Supercan on an old sawhorse, he could make him go through the rowing motions. But rowing should really be done in water, and to make Supercan row in the turkey shed was hard on both oars and dirt floor. One could always do arithmetic problems, but even they get tiresome after a while.

Bucket was of no use at all. Plenty of water fell outside, but inside the shed there was absolutely nothing for a robot to dip up and pour. Besides, both of the big robots' batteries were running down and needed recharging. The two tin men worked more and more slowly, and presently even Supercan's bell jangled incorrect answers to the arithmetic problems.

If Andy pressed the five-by-five buttons, instead of getting twenty-five jingles, he might get eighteen or thirteen or some careless answer. It was all very disappointing, on a dark day with rain pelting on the roof, to have the mechanical things go wrong too.

Andy sighed. He dusted and oiled the tin men, so that they would not rust, and put them back against the wall. He did not even bother to tell them good-by. He simply turned his back on them, closed the turkey-shed door, and sloshed down to the farmhouse for supper.

With so much rain the river began to rise. It crept up over the dock, and Mrs. Buckram began to be worried.

"What if we have a flood?" she asked.

"We haven't had a flood in years, my dear," said Mr. Buckram. "There's absolutely no need to get nervous."

The river kept rising until it was almost in the barnyard, and still it rained. Strange things began to go by on the river, chicken coops and parts of strawstacks and old boats that had not been properly anchored.

"It really looks like a flood, doesn't it, Clyde?" asked Mrs. Buckram anxiously. "Hadn't we better go up to Uncle Edwin's place on higher ground?"

"Now, Milly, you know it's too early for the rainy season, and we haven't had a flood in twenty years. I'm sure that the sun will be shining tomorrow," Andy's father said cheerfully.

Andy did not say anything, but he thought that a flood might be exciting. He felt glad that the robots were safe on high ground.

One night after they had gone to bed came the worst storm of all. Rain fell in sheets, the thunder rolled like artillery guns, and the lightning flashed up and down the river.

Andy lay in bed listening. It was after midnight, but in the uproar of the storm he could not sleep. Andy began to count the number of seconds between the flash of lightning and the crash of thunder. He knew that light travels much faster than sound. It may take light many thousands of years to travel from a distant star, but it is a different matter with a flash of lightning which strikes within a few miles of home. Here, close by, the light is seen just as the lightning strikes. But the sound travels only about a mile in five

83

seconds. So, by counting seconds after he saw the flash of light, Andy could tell approximately how far away it had struck.

Now he counted twelve seconds between the flash and the crash. He divided twelve by five and decided that the lightning must have struck about two and four-tenths miles away.

"Gee!" Andy said to himself, "That's getting pretty close." He heard his parents talking and moving about in the kitchen, and presently Andy got up and pulled on his clothes.

"It's really a rip-snorter of a storm, Andy," Mr. Buckram said. "We were just going to call you."

Andy's parents were both dressed, and Mrs. Buckram had begun to make sandwiches, as if she intended to go on a picnic. "I just hope the lightning doesn't strike us before we get to Uncle Edwin's," she said.

"Are we going to Uncle Edwin's?" asked Andy.

"Yes," said Mr. Buckram. "Your mother was right, as she very often is, Andy. We should have gone up to Uncle Edwin's yesterday morning, when your mother first suggested it."

Mrs. Buckram did not say anything. She was so busy packing lunches and gathering valuable things together that she did not even give herself the pleasure of saying, "I told you so."

Another flash of lightning ripped across the sky, and Andy counted ten before he heard the thunder.

"It's coming closer," he said.

"We'll have to hurry, Andy," said Mr. Buckram. "While I hitch the horses to the wagon and let the cows out of their stalls, I want you to open up the chicken yards and pigpens so that the animals can save themselves in case the barnyard is flooded. Then come right back, and we'll drive to Uncle Edwin's."

"Put on your raincoat and rubber boots, Andy," his mother said, "and, here, put this packet of sandwiches into your pocket. We don't want to eat Uncle Edwin out of house and home. If each person carries his own lunch, we shall not need the heavy picnic basket."

"Why can't I take my school lunch box with milk in the Thermos bottle?" asked Andy. "I can get it into the big pocket of my raincoat. I've done it lots of times."

"Very well," Mrs. Buckram said, "but hurry. I don't think we have much time."

Andy was amazed to see by the light from the doorway that dark water lapped and splashed right around the foundation of the farmhouse. He saw his father with a flashlight wading across the farmyard toward the barn. Andy took his own flashlight and splashed away toward the chicken yard and the pigpen.

A great glare of lightning suddenly illuminated the whole scene, and it looked as if the river were all around them. House and barn jutted up very strangely like islands in the rushing water. Automatically Andy counted the seconds

before the clap of thunder, but there were only four. The lightning must have struck less than a mile away.

Andy ran to the chicken yard first and shooed out the surprised and frightened chickens. They began squawking and fluttering up into trees.

Next he herded the pigs out of their pen and chased them toward higher ground. They squealed as if all the robots in the world were after them, but this was not the moment to stop and give them their tranquilizing pills.

"Run! run! run!" shouted Andy. "Save yourselves if you can."

He could see that the water was rising higher every moment, and he ran as fast as he could back toward the farmhouse. Before he reached it, however, another flash of lightning came, followed almost immediately by thunder. As plain as day Andy saw the little turkey shed at the top of the hill under the big pine tree.

"Oh, my robots!" Andy cried. "My wonderful tin men!" After all the work and time and skill he had spent on them, Andy could not bear to leave them to the flood. "I'm sure I can put them into the back of the wagon," he thought.

He could hear the water roaring below him in a new fury as he climbed toward the turkey shed. He knew that he did not have a moment to lose.

"Andy! Andy!" his mother and father were calling. He could see them standing together in the lighted doorway of the farmhouse below. The water rushed past them in the lamplight.

"Just a minute," Andy called. "Just a little, small second!"

At the same instant there came the most terrible clap of thunder that Andy had yet heard. A blinding light flashed all around him, and some terrific force knocked him flat on the ground. He could hear a grinding and crashing sound, and the roaring of water and splitting of timber.

For a moment Andy lay still, unable to remember where he was or what had happened. Then he struggled to his feet, calling, "Daddy! Mama!"

But when he looked back to the farmyard the electric lights had all gone out, and it seemed to his excited imagination that the dark bulk of his house was moving and bobbing and floating away. The barn too—surely it was sailing away like a great ship!

Everything had become pitch dark after the last terrific flash of lightning. The water began to lap around Andy's boots again, and he knew that he must continue to climb up the hill to get away from it. As he struggled upward, he began to notice that it was not quite so dark ahead of him. A quiet light came from the cracks of the old turkey house. The shed was certainly not afire, but a subdued glow came from it. It was the sort of glow that might have been made by Christmas-tree lights or flashlight bulbs without reflectors.

In this soft glow Andy could see that the giant pine tree had been split in two by the lightning, but the shed did not seem to be damaged at all. He stood there staring at it until he felt the water lapping about his feet.

Then he started to climb again, and in the lull between claps of thunder he heard a new strange noise. It was not the roar of water or the splintering of timber. It was the sound of a voice.

"Ha! ha! ha! ha! ha! Ho! ho! ho! ho! ho!" laughed the

voice, and then it let out the jolliest kind of yodel. "Yo-lally! yo-lally! yo!"

"Lily Belle!" shrieked Andy. "Great frogs and catfish! What is going on here?"

He ran to the door of the turkey shed and threw it open. Out of the darkness eight glowing eyes were staring at him. The robots had all been electrified by the lightning! They looked at him with round, bright eyes.

"Well, master, what next?" they seemed to be saying to him.

On the River

Andy did not have time to marvel at what had happened. He stepped into the turkey house and found that it was still dry. Campbell came limping over to him and held up his arms to be taken.

"Not now, Campbell, but I'll do the best I can for you," Andy said. "I'll try to save all of you if I can. But we'll have to get to higher ground in a hurry. The water is still rising."

The other three robots also came and stood around him, expecting him to help them. Andy scratched his head in perplexity. They certainly seemed to be working perfectly, but he did not know how much he could count on them.

"You'll have to walk," he said, "even Campbell and Lily Belle. We are almost at the top of the hill. If we can get out into open country before the river completely overflows its banks and floods the countryside, maybe we can keep ahead of it and get to Uncle Edwin's."

Supercan's little bell began jangling frantically, and Bucket's pails were clanging and clashing. Lily Belle roared, "Help! help! help!" and Andy had to slap her on the back to make her stop it.

Andy went to the door of the turkey shed and flashed his light outside and up the final slope of the hill to see if they could still climb to safety. But the river had already reached the back of the turkey shed, cutting off their retreat. Even inside the shed, Andy could see that water was seeping in under the foundation and oozing across the dirt floor. If the shed was swept off its foundation, there would be no floor to protect them. They would all be left at the mercy of the flood.

Campbell kept holding up his arms to Andy very piteously, as much as to say, "Papa, you got us into this, now please to rescue us."

Lily Belle was singing now in a very sad voice, "Down will come rockabye baby and all," and Supercan was ringing and flashing and rattling in a very agitated manner.

In the circumstances Bucket showed the most sense of any of them. He began to dip up the water that seeped in and rose about their feet, and to throw it out the turkey-house door. Unfortunately water ran back as fast as Bucket threw it out.

There came another flash of lightning, and, before the clap of thunder, Andy could hear Supercan's little bell ringing one-two-three-four-five. At "five" came the clap of thunder. Andy looked at Supercan and saw that he had begun to calm down. Was he counting to some purpose now?

"Well," Andy said, "at least the lightning is striking farther away. Thank goodness for that!"

Just then something bumped into a corner of the turkey shed, and Andy looked out and flashed his torch. There was the boat! It was still upside down, but it had floated up from the sawhorses on which it had been resting, and now it bumped gently against the corner of the shed. Andy leaned out the door until he could touch the boat.

"Oh, boat! Lovely *Dorinda!* You never looked so good to me," he said. He caught hold of it and pulled it up to the turkey-house door. But the current of the water also pulled at it, and he found that he could not turn the boat over. He had only enough strength to hang onto it and to keep it from drifting away.

Behind him, Andy heard Supercan's little bell ringing, ding-dong, ding-dong. It irritated him, and he cried out, "Well, you big hunk of tin, if you were really a supercan you would help me to turn over this boat."

He really did not expect any help from Supercan, but

suddenly he felt the boat being lifted out of the water and turned over by a pair of very strong arms. To Andy's amazement the boat was turned neatly right side up and floating safely in front of the turkey-shed door, and Supercan was helping him to hold it there.

"Supercan, you did it!" Andy cried in delight. Supercan's bell jangled excitedly, and he seemed to be satisfied with his accomplishment.

Just then something nudged Andy from behind, and, looking around, he saw that Lily Belle had dragged the oars and the steering paddle out from the corner of the shed and was holding them in readiness.

"Ho! ho! ho! ho! ho!" laughed Lily Belle delightedly.

Andy had no time to praise her. The water was rising higher and higher. At any moment now the turkey shed might be washed away. He grabbed the oars and paddle and threw them into the boat.

"Get in!" he ordered. "All of you, get in!"

Instantly the robots began to clamber into the boat. While they had no minds of their own, Andy began to see that, in their new state of electrification, they were able to obey commands.

"Steady," Andy said. "Look out you don't tip it. Sit down quietly as soon as you are in."

Andy had to help Lily Belle, who laughed and yodeled excitedly and was far too fat for her legs. Campbell came up last, and for once he did not hold up his arms for help. Andy saw that he was dragging something behind him. It

93

turned out to be the ax that Mr. Buckram kept in a corner of the shed.

"Who knows? It may be useful," said Andy, tossing it into the boat. At that Campbell held up his arms in the usual way, and Andy lifted him in beside the other robots. Bucket and Supercan looked out for themselves. As a matter of course Supercan sat down on the rower's seat, and Andy clamped the oars into his hands.

"I'll sit in the stern and steer with the paddle," Andy said. "Now push off, Supercan. Get away from the turkey shed before it breaks loose and hits us."

With a mighty thrust of the oars, Supercan pushed off and began to row. In a moment they were safely away on the crest of the flood.

The job of steering was a very difficult one. By this time houses and parts of haystacks and broken trees were floating down the flooded river. In the darkness Andy could see only a short distance ahead. He did not know in which direction they were going, but he tried to steer clear of dangerous objects which might capsize the boat. He was so busy steering that he scarcely thought about how *Dorinda* might leak. Only when he felt water about his feet did he remember.

Oh, if only he had calked and painted the boat earlier in the summer! Now, with the added weight of the robots, it leaked quite dangerously.

"Bucket," Andy shouted, "you will have to bail."

Bucket began to obey so vigorously that he almost upset the boat.

"Gently! Carefully, Bucket!" Andy shouted. It took a little time, but gradually Bucket settled into a quiet routine of bailing and emptying water over the side.

"Good Bucket!" Andy cried. "Good Supercan!" For Supercan was rowing steadily and surely now. With every forward motion of his body, his little bell tolled, and Andy thought hopefully that it sounded very much like a bell buoy and should warn away other boats in the darkness. The two biggest tin men were performing beautifully.

"Great frogs and catfish!" Andy said to himself. "This is almost too good to be true. I hope they can keep it up." He thought that if they could reach Grandpa Clayton's house they would be able to get help, and perhaps they could find out what had happened to his father and mother. But now he worried that they might pass the Automobile Graveyard in the darkness without seeing it.

The rain fell less heavily now, and the thunder and lightning sounded far away. But beneath them the angry river eddied and swirled, and it was an ever-present danger. If *Dorinda* could only hold together until they reached some temporary safety! Andy managed to keep clear of floating objects, but he had no way of knowing whether or not he was steering in the right direction to reach the Graveyard.

Dimly Andy could see that Campbell had climbed onto Lily Belle's lap, and he could hear her singing to him.

95

"Well, what else could you expect?" he asked himself disgustedly. At least Supercan and Bucket behaved like brave men, and he hoped that they would see him through this terrible night.

At last the pale light of dawn began to break over a scene of great desolation. It had completely stopped raining now, but the river was so swollen that the familiar landmarks were all changed. Trees that had been high on the bank now stood half submerged in water. Andy could not tell where he was. Unless they had been rowing in circles, as he had sometimes felt that they might be, Andy feared they had already passed Grandpa Clayton's place in the darkness. He kept thinking about Sparrow and wondering if she and her grandfather had reached a safe spot, or if they too were adrift on the river.

About this time he began to see a number of queer objects like small islands sticking out of the water. As he steered around one of them, Andy suddenly discovered it to be the top of an old automobile which was nearly submerged in the river.

"The Graveyard!" Andy cried. "It must be the Graveyard!" Between the tops of old cars floated the loose parts and pieces which Andy had always found such a delight at Grandpa Clayton's place. Spare tires and old fenders, bits of rope, and pieces of tin were floating merrily away to the sea.

Andy was so busy keeping the boat from crashing into floating objects, that he did not at first see the roof of

Grandpa Clayton's shanty sticking out of the water. Lily Belle saw it first and began to roar, "Help! help! help!" and point toward the roof of the house. Then Andy noticed it, and he saw that someone was sitting on top of the roof.

"Sparrow!" Andy shouted. "Sparrow!"

"Oh, Andy!" Sparrow shouted back. "I thought you'd never come!"

Sparrow had on her raincoat and hat and rubber boots, and she clutched her lunch kit in her hands. She looked quite calm and as if she were only waiting for the school bus to come by and pick her up. In fact she seemed much calmer than Lily Belle, who still yelled, "Help! Help! Help!" All the same, Andy could see that Sparrow was pale, and he knew that she must be frightened.

"Hush up, Lily Belle," Andy said as the boat came up beside Sparrow's roof. "Now, ease down on the oars, Supercan. Slow, now. Easy does it! We don't want to capsize the boat. Keep on bailing, Bucket. One more passenger will make our load heavier. Come on now, Sparrow, you'll have to jump for it."

"Oh, Andy, I don't know if I can," Sparrow said. "I'll have to shut my eyes."

"Don't be silly," Andy said. "How can you see where to jump if you shut your eyes? Look what you're doing and jump quick. We can't hold the boat here all day."

"Oh, dear! Oh, dear!" wailed Sparrow. "I can't do it. Really, I can't!"

Out of the corner of his eye Andy could see a large

piece of picket fence bearing down upon them. In another
moment it would strike the boat and whirl them away from
Sparrow's roof. If they were not actually capsized, it
seemed at least likely that they would never be able to get
back within reach of Sparrow's roof again.

"Jump!" yelled Andy at the top of his lungs. His voice
sounded so loud and commanding that Sparrow was

startled and surprised into jumping right into the boat. Everything worked out perfectly, and in a moment she was sitting beside Lily Belle and Campbell, as if she had always been there.

But now, of all times, when she was safe in the boat, Sparrow began to cry. "Oh, dear! Oh, dear!" she said, and then again, "Oh, dear!"

More Passengers

"Listen, Sparrow," Andy said, "it doesn't help a bit to cry. What you need is breakfast. I've got some sandwiches and a Thermos of milk in my pocket. You may have some of that."

"I have my own lunch," Sparrow said as she opened her lunch pail. "Grandpa told me to put as much food into it as I could."

"Where is your Grandpa?" Andy asked.

"Oh, I don't know," said Sparrow, ready to cry again. "It all happened so fast. We woke up and found the flood all around our house, and we had to hurry, and it was very confusing."

"It sure was," Andy said, remembering his own experience.

"Grandpa told me to get the food ready, and he would bring the boat around to the door. I waited for him there, and I could see him coming in the boat. But before he got near me part of an old bridge came floating between the boat and the house. The current was so strong it kept sweeping him farther and farther away. I could see the boat being carried away in spite of all he could do. Then Grandpa stood up in the boat and shouted to me. 'Get on the roof, Sparrow,' he shouted. 'Take care of yourself. I can't help you!' "

"And that's the last you saw of him?"

"Yes, it was so dark, and when the next flash of lightning came I couldn't see the boat any more at all. So I climbed on the roof and sat and waited. I hoped maybe you would come."

"Well, I'm glad I did," Andy said.

"And what about your parents, Andy?"

"They are gone too," Andy said. "I saw them standing in the doorway of the house, calling to me. And then the house lights went out and the house was swept away by the flood."

"And where were you?"

"I was going up the hill to rescue my robots."

"I see that you did," Sparrow said. She looked around at the robots now, as if she were noticing them for the first time. "Good land!" she cried. "How come they are working and not plugged in?"

"I think the lightning did it," Andy said. "I don't know any other reason for it. They were in the turkey shed, you know, and even the batteries in Supercan and Bucket were all run down so they could hardly move. But when lightning struck the big pine tree it seemed to run all through the turkey house. By the time I got there the robots were like this."

"For goodness' sake! But how did you get them into the boat all by yourself and set them all to working? I remember what a time we had that day in your kitchen."

"That's the wonderful thing," Andy said. "Now they do whatever I order them to do. I don't have to touch the controls. All they need to know is what is expected of them, and they go ahead and do it. Supercan helped me to turn the boat over and hold it while everyone got in, and you see how he is rowing and how Bucket is bailing. I couldn't have done it alone."

"For goodness' sake!" Sparrow said again.

Just then Lily Belle began to laugh. "Ha! ha! ha! ha! ha! Ho! ho! ho! ho! ho!"

"Did you want her to do that?" Sparrow asked.

"Well, no," Andy admitted. "Sometimes Lily Belle gets out of hand. She's quite a nuisance. Be still, Lily Belle."

"Let her laugh," said Sparrow. "It's nice to know that someone thinks this flood is funny. I certainly don't. But I'd rather hear Lily Belle laughing than myself crying."

"I thought you were going to eat your breakfast," Andy said. "You'll feel better when you do."

Sparrow took a peanut-butter sandwich out of her lunch kit and began to eat it. The robots all turned their heads and looked at her, and she stopped in the middle of a bite and stared back at them. She had a very guilty feeling that she must be snatching food out of their mouths. "Andy, do you think they are hungry? Will they eat now, like we do? Should I give Campbell a sandwich?"

"I hope they won't eat," Andy said. "We may not have enough for ourselves until we get help. But maybe you had better try them."

Sparrow broke off a small piece of sandwich and handed it to Campbell. He passed it to Lily Belle, who passed it to Bucket, who passed it to Supercan, who passed it back to Campbell, who passed it back to Sparrow. The robots did not know what to do with it.

"It's just as well," Andy said. "Eat it yourself, Sparrow, and then you can change seats with me and steer while I eat my breakfast."

"They really are marvelous," said Sparrow. She looked admiringly at the tin men as she munched her sandwich.

"Yes," said Andy, "I'm proud of them. We'd have had a hard time of it if Supercan had not rowed and Bucket bailed."

"And if Lily Belle hadn't laughed," added Sparrow. "They're all useful, Andy."

"All except Campbell," said Andy. "Poor baby, he never could do anything useful."

Campbell sat very close to Lily Belle and hung his head.

"Don't say things like that before him, Andy," cautioned Sparrow. "I think he understands and is ashamed."

"Well, it isn't his fault, it's mine," Andy said. "I didn't know how to build a good robot when I made him. I don't blame him. I blame myself."

"I'll steer now while you eat, Andy. But what are we going to do? What is to become of us?"

They changed seats, and Andy said cheerfully, "The main thing now is to keep clear of floating logs and chicken coops. I wish we had a compass to tell which way we are going. If the sun would come out, I could get our bearings and steer for Riverdale. That should be the next town downriver. Maybe we'll find our folks there."

"At the rate we're going," said Sparrow, "the river will sweep us right out to sea before we ever come in sight of a town."

"The sea is a long way off yet," said Andy, "but do you remember that big island that used to stick way up out of the water at the place where the river widened on the way to Riverdale? Sometimes we used to have Fourth of July picnics there. If it hasn't been flooded or washed away, we might be able to land on that. It seems as if there must be something besides water left in all this world."

It really did not look as if there were. Under the heavy skies water spread around them on all sides. Sometimes a barn roof or a tree or a telephone pole stuck up out of it, but except for those the river might as well have been the ocean. Not a living thing could be seen—not even a bird flying overhead. Odd wreckage kept floating down the river beside them. There were empty barrels and pieces of fence and broken gates.

"If we all get out of this alive and reach home again," Andy said, "your grandpa ought to be able to collect a fine lot of junk."

"Yes," Sparrow said sadly. Her sandwich had not cheered her as much as Andy had hoped. Even Lily Belle had stopped laughing, and Supercan's bell sounded more like a knell than a jolly tinkle.

"If only we knew which direction to take!" Andy said. "If we could only see some living thing!"

So they went on as best they could, rowing back and forth to avoid floating objects, and being carried by the force of the flood.

Finally, in the midst of the gloomy silence which had fallen upon them, Sparrow said, "Listen! I think I hear something."

"It's me, swallowing my sandwich," Andy said.

"No, it's a dog barking. I'm sure. Listen!"

The robots all turned their heads in the direction of the sound, and Andy heard it too. Far away a dog was barking.

"Let me steer," Andy said. "We'll go for it as fast as we can. Where there are dogs, there are people."

Supercan rowed harder than ever, and Bucket bailed.

Andy steered toward the barkings of the dog. Still they could not see land, only queer things floating on the water. But the sound of barking gradually grew louder.

"It sounds like Tiddley," Andy said.

"Who's Tiddley?"

"Tiddley is Cousin Eva's dog. But Cousin Eva lives way up the river, beyond our place. It couldn't be Tiddley, unless—"

"Andy, it isn't land," Sparrow said. "It's just something floating, and there's a dog on it. There's something else on it too."

"I see," said Andy. "It looks like a barn door, and there's a dog, and there's a—there's a— Oh, no!"

"What's an O-no, Andy?" asked Sparrow. "It looks like a baby to me, a darling little girl baby floating on a barn door."

Just then Lily Belle began to sing in a loud, happy voice,

"Rockabye, baby, on the treetop,
When the wind blows—"

"Hush up, Lily Belle," Andy said rudely. "You'd better scream, 'Help,' because we're going to need it. That's Cousin Eva's Dot!"

"Oh, the poor baby!" cried Sparrow, and Campbell nearly fell overboard trying to reach his arm toward the baby on the barn door.

"Look out, Campbell. Don't get in the way," commanded Andy. "Of course we'll have to save her. But of

all the people in the world that we might have had a chance to save, why did it have to be Dot?"

"She looks adorable to me," Sparrow said, and Lily Belle, in Senator Quackenbush's voice, roared, "There is great cause for rejoicing."

"Well, I hope so," Andy said as he steered the boat alongside the barn door. "Easy, now. Just hold the boat steady, Supercan. All hands prepare to take on passengers."

As soon as Tiddley saw them he stopped barking and began to whine and wag his tail. Dot sat up straight in the middle of the barn door, clutching her "b'anky" and sucking her thumb. She looked at them with wide, hostile blue eyes. She did not seem as pleased to see them as Tiddley was.

"Hello, Dot," said Andy very kindly.

"No, no, no!" said Dot in a good strong voice.

"Nice baby," Andy said, "be good now. Nice Andy has come to help little Dottie."

"No, no, no," said Dot.

"She doesn't want to be helped, Andy," Sparrow said.

"She never does," said Andy, "but we'll just have to get her into the boat, whether she wants it or not. We can't let Cousin Eva's baby float out to sea on a barn door, no matter how horrid she is."

"I think I can get her, Andy. You and Supercan keep the boat steady. I'm sure I can reach her." Sparrow stretched out her arms and caught hold of Dot's coat. At this Dot began to scream and struggle as if she were in the hands of kidnapers.

On hearing this, Tiddley grew very excited. He did not know who was being bad to whom. He had hoped very much that they were all friends, but, with Dot struggling and screaming, he could not tell who was a friend and who was an enemy. Now he jumped into the boat and back again onto the barn-door raft, and into the boat and back to the barn door.

Bucket tried to put a pail over Tiddley's head, and Tiddley tried to bite Bucket on the leg. The poor little dog was more confused than ever when he found that he was biting tin.

And all the while Dot screamed, "No. No. No. I-da-wa-na. I-da-wa-na. No. No. No." But finally Sparrow and Andy succeeded in hauling her into the boat. Sparrow tried to hold her, but Dot kicked and screamed and beat her fists against Sparrow's chest and her heels against the side of the boat. The boat rocked dangerously, and the barn door went floating away.

"Look out, she'll overturn the boat," Andy cried. "Dot, behave yourself!"

"No! No! No!" howled Dot.

"Maybe we should have left her where she was," Sparrow said. "But I really didn't see much future for her on a barn door."

"There may not be very much future for any of us, in a leaky boat, if she behaves like this," Andy said.

It was a grim moment, and nobody felt like laughing. Nobody, that is, except Lily Belle. Suddenly she began to rock and howl with laughter. "Ha! ha! ha! ha! Ho! ho! ho! ho! ho!"

Andy was about to say, "Shut up, Lily Belle," in his very rudest manner, when he noticed that Dot had stopped screaming. She stopped beating her hands and kicking her heels, and then she began to laugh too.

Campbell was sitting on Lily Belle's lap, and now Dot toddled over and shoved him off.

"Ha! ha! ha!" she said. "Me! Me!" And up she climbed onto Lily Belle's lap and put her head back against Lily Belle's tin shoulder. The boat stopped rocking, Tiddley began to wag and smile, Supercan rowed, and Bucket bailed. A wonderful peace and quiet settled down upon the *Dorinda*.

There was no use asking Dot how she and Tiddley happened to be floating on a barn door, alone on the flooded river. She probably would not have told them if she could. She wore her coat and bonnet, as if her mother had been getting ready to take her to higher ground. But here she was now with Andy and Sparrow and the robots in a leaky boat. She looked tired and hungry, but at least she was no longer cross. While Lily Belle held her and laughed and yodeled, Sparrow managed to feed her some milk and sandwich.

Campbell stood by and looked at Dot, and he was the only one who did not seem pleased with the way things had turned out. He had lost his comfortable seat on Lily Belle's lap to another baby, and he did not know what to do about it.

"It's all right, Campbell," Sparrow said. "You can sit on my lap, honey."

"Great frogs and catfish!" said Andy in disgust. "Even

in the midst of a flood, girls are girls and babies are babies."

"And what is wrong about that, please?" asked Sparrow haughtily. "Do you want us to turn into angleworms?"

Campbell did not accept Sparrow's kind offer but sat down shyly by himself with his head hanging.

"Look, darling," Sparrow coaxed him, "here's my hanky, and you can use it for a b'anky."

"Hanky! B'anky!" Andy mocked. But Campbell accepted Sparrow's handkerchief and pressed it against his cheek.

"There, dear," Sparrow said, "and I do think that Andy might have given you a thumb to suck. But we love you anyway, and everything is going to be all right."

"I hope it is!" said Andy to himself. After all, he was the one who was responsible for the safety of all of them.

"Be Joyful, Tin Men!"

Before noon the sun suddenly came out. The fog lifted from the river, and the children could begin to see where they were. On either side of the vast expanse of water, pine-covered bluffs appeared in the distance. Before water had covered all the flat land, these had been the faraway hills.

"And there," cried Andy, "there's the island! The big island in the river where we used to have Fourth of July picnics!" He began to feel much more cheerful.

Just ahead of them the island looked solid and inviting. It was the nearest bit of land, and Andy began to steer toward it. "I always wanted to camp on that island," Andy said. "Maybe now—"

"But it used to have a nice sand beach," Sparrow said. "I remember it very well."

"Don't forget how high the water is," said Andy. "The sand beach must be under water. All that's left uncovered are rocks and trees."

"Still, it's land," Sparrow said, "and it certainly looks good to me."

As if the robots understood, Supercan began to row harder, and Bucket began to bail more energetically. The harder he bailed, however, the more the water seemed to be leaking into the boat.

"It's getting awfully wet!" Andy said. "I think he's wearing a hole in the bottom of the boat. Don't bail so hard, Bucket."

But when Bucket bailed more slowly the water came up around their feet. *Dorinda* was certainly a mess and bound to sink if they did not reach the island soon.

"All right, row hard! Bail hard!" Andy shouted. "If we can't make it in the boat, we'll just have to swim for the island."

"What about me?" Sparrow cried. "I'm not a very good swimmer. What about Dot and the robots?"

"Don't ask so many questions," Andy said. "We're almost there. Get ready to jump if you have to."

Supercan rowed like mad, and the boat shot through the water now at top speed. Andy kept her headed directly for the island, and the two children watched anxiously as the strip of water between themselves and the island grew narrower and narrower.

"Oh, Andy, we're going to make it! We are!" Sparrow cried, and just in time Andy shouted, "Stop rowing! Stop bailing!"—before the robots drove the boat right into the rocky side of the shore. There was a grating, ripping sound, and the boat came to a sudden stop.

"Yo-lally! Yo-lally!" cried Lily Belle, and Andy let out a yell of triumph. But the next moment he began to groan. A rock, projecting from the submerged island, had made a long gash in the bottom of the boat. The water poured in now in earnest. But the children scrambled to safety and pulled the boat above the waterline.

"Whew!" cried Andy. "That was close." He grabbed Dot and swung her onto shore, and, barking with delight, Tiddley jumped out after her. But the robots continued to sit in the wrecked boat, awaiting further instructions.

"Well, get out, you stupid tin men!" Andy shouted.

"You might at least be polite to them, Andy," said Sparrow. "Remember who rowed and bailed for us. Where would we be without them?"

"I know," Andy said. "I didn't mean to sound cross. But you'd think they would be a little joyful instead of just sitting there."

"I don't think they know how to be joyful, Andy. They just do what they are told to do."

"Well, then I'll tell them what to do. Be joyful, tin men, be joyful!" Looking very puzzled, the robots climbed out

of the boat. They really did not know how to be joyful.

"Look!" Sparrow cried. "Like this, dears!" She began to caper and dance and wave her hands. The bewildered robots followed her example and capered solemnly around and around without a glint of pleasure. Only Lily Belle sounded joyful. "Ha! ha! ha!" she laughed.

"Good robots," said Sparrow. "See, Andy, they are doing their best."

"Okay," said Andy. "That will do for being joyful. Now we'll have to get to work." At the word "work," the robots looked more cheerful. They understood that better than being joyful. They came and stood around Andy, waiting for instructions. Andy drew a long breath. He began to remember all the times he had longed to go camping in the woods. His father had promised that he would take him, but there were always too many chores to do on the farm, and so Andy had gone on sleeping in a clean room with a good roof over his head when he might have been living in the open.

"Oh boy!" he said. "Now we can begin to live."

"How do you mean?" asked Sparrow. "It looks pretty bleak to me."

"We'll build a wonderful camp," Andy cried. "We'll all have a chance to rough it." Sparrow did not feel so sure that roughing it was a good thing, but then, she had never longed to go camping as Andy had.

"How about the boat?" she asked.

"Oh, we'll have to mend the boat," Andy said. "But first we'll select a good level campsite, and we'll cut dry wood for a fire and green branches for beds and saplings for a wickiup—"

"A wickiwhat?" asked Sparrow nervously.

"A wickiup. Don't you know what that is? It's a shelter of branches that the Indians build. I read just how to build one in *The Boy's Popular Mechanics Magazine*. After we get our campfire, we'll have to boil our water so it won't make us sick to drink it. When everything is done, we'll be very snug here, and we can safely stay until snow flies."

"Until snow flies?" cried Sparrow in dismay. "You sound as if you planned to settle down here."

"Sparrow, you don't realize what a wonderful opportunity this is," said Andy. Sparrow realized all too well, but it did not seem so wonderful to her as it did to Andy.

"Don't you think that someone might come by and rescue us before snow flies?" she asked wistfully.

"Oh, sure," Andy said. "Sometime we'll be rescued, but in the meantime I'm going to have a lot of fun setting up a real good camp."

"And what shall we eat?" asked Sparrow.

Andy thought for a moment. "I'll put you in charge of food, Sparrow," he said generously. "After all, I don't want to take all the good jobs. I want you to have some fun too."

"But our lunch kits are nearly empty," protested Sparrow, "and we are sure to be hungry soon. Where shall I find food?"

"Use your head, Sparrow," said Andy. He was very eager to get started on the wickiup.

"My head?" cried Sparrow in dismay.

"Listen," said Andy patiently, "at this time of year there are sure to be blackberries or nuts on the island. And when I've set up a good camp I'll catch some fish."

"But how?" asked Sparrow. "We don't have any fishing poles or lines or hooks."

"Well, I'll build a fish trap. I never found anything I couldn't invent if I tried."

"I know you're a very inventive boy, Andy. But you usually have a lot of screws and bolts and solder and spare parts. Here you don't have any of those things—unless you take the robots apart."

Andy looked at the robots and shook his head. "I couldn't do that," he said slowly. "They—they're almost human."

"Oh, I didn't really mean that you *should* take them apart," Sparrow cried. "I love them all too much for that, especially Campbell."

"And, of course, we'll need them," Andy said. "I'm going to make them work for us."

"What will you make them do?"

"Why, Supercan and Bucket and I will start cutting wood for a fire and for beds and for the wickiup—"

"With what?" asked Sparrow, who liked everything explained.

"With the ax Campbell brought, of course," Andy said. "It's in the bottom of the boat."

"Do you mean to tell me that Campbell did a smart thing like bringing an ax, and you haven't praised him for it?"

"Well, it *was* a smart thing to do," Andy said, "for a baby. It was probably an accident, but thank you anyway, Campbell."

Campbell came and put up his arms to be lifted and

118

kissed, but that was a little too much for Andy. "Let's just shake hands, Campbell," he said. "Thank you again, old man."

"And what about Lily Belle?" asked Sparrow.

"Before you start out hunting food," Andy said, "you can set Lily Belle to rubbing sticks together to make a fire. We don't have any matches, and robots don't get tired. That will be a fine job for Lily Belle."

Andy started right to work, showing the two large robots what he wanted them to do. With a little help and teaching, it turned out that Supercan could chop as well as row. Andy figured that in an hour or so he and Supercan would have chopped enough dry wood for the fire and green wood for the wickiup and the beds. He unhooked the buckets from the ends of Bucket's arms, and Bucket soon learned to use his hooks to lift and drag the trees and branches and put them into neat piles where Andy wanted them.

Sparrow watched all this activity for a moment, and she tried to be as cheerful as Andy seemed to be. She could see that he was already having a lot of fun. She drew a long sigh before she turned to her own work. But first she seated Lily Belle on a fallen log and gave her two sticks to rub together.

"Take this, Lily Belle. See? Rub, rub, rub, and after a while you will get a spark." Unfortunately Sparrow did not think to tell Lily Belle what to do with the spark when she got it.

Instead Sparrow was thinking about the problem of finding food. She began to feel hungry herself, and Dot had started to say, "Cook-ky," and, "D'ink." Sparrow knew that when the baby became a little hungrier she would make a scene. First, Sparrow examined her lunch kit and found that she had only a very little milk left in the Thermos bottle. She also had half of a peanut-butter sandwich. She gave Dot the rest of the milk to keep her happy as long as possible. The half-sandwich, wrapped in waxed paper, she put in her pocket. As she did so, Sparrow discovered that she had something else in her pocket as well. She brought it out and looked at it. It was a single stick of Doublemint gum.

"Well, that won't keep anyone from starvation," she said to herself, and she was about to put it into her mouth. It would have been very comforting at that moment to be chewing a nice fresh stick of Doublemint gum. But then she thought, "No, I'd better save it. Things may get worse before they get better, and I might need it more later." Reluctantly she put it back into her pocket.

Now that the sun had come out strong and warm, the island steamed and sparkled. Every wet leaf glistened, and sky and river were beautifully blue.

"What a day for a picnic," Sparrow said to herself, "if only we had a lunch!" The lunch was the problem, and she knew that she had better get busy and look for it. She decided that she would climb up through the woods and see if Andy was right about blackberries or nuts. The woods should be full of them at this season of the year.

It would have been easy and pleasant to go by herself, but Andy was busy, and she dared not leave Dot alone. So she took Dot by one hand and Campbell by the other and began to climb up toward the top of the island. Tiddley went along too, and he soon occupied himself by chasing birds and rabbits and squirrels.

It seemed to Sparrow that there were more birds and rabbits and squirrels than she had ever seen in one place before. At first this seemed strange, until it occurred to her that all these wild creatures must have taken shelter on the island because they could find no other place to go in the flood.

"They are just like us," she thought. "They flew or swam here to save themselves. I wonder if any of the farm animals could have reached the island too."

Tiddley dashed here and there among the ferns and bushes, following mysterious little rustlings and scurryings, and presently he disappeared entirely. It was very slow going with Dot and Campbell, but Dot seemed cheerful and good-tempered. With the last of Sparrow's milk inside her, she was quite pleased to toddle along and explore the island.

After a while the trees seemed to be thinning out, and Sparrow could see sunlight falling on an open meadow. She knew that berries often grow in such open places in the woods. She picked Dot up and carried her so that they could go more quickly. As they came out of the trees they were rewarded by the sight of many berry bushes growing in the sunlight. There were ripe berries hanging on the bushes too. This was easier than Sparrow had expected.

"Why didn't I bring one of Bucket's pails?" she thought. "I'll have to go back. But first we'll eat a few ourselves."

She picked a berry and found it good and sweet and juicy. The next one she popped into Dot's mouth, and Dot was pleased. Instead of saying, "I-da-wa-na," she said, "Mo'!" and opened her mouth like a baby bird. After that most of the berries went into Dot, but, with so many bushes, Sparrow did not feel concerned about the number of berries that would be left.

But as they worked themselves farther into the patch Sparrow changed her mind about the supply of fruit. The berries thinned out rapidly, and toward the center of the clearing they certainly had been picked and the bushes trampled down. Someone must have come in from the other side of the island and picked berries before them.

"That's funny," Sparrow said to herself. "It looks as if we aren't the only berry-eaters on this island. Could there be other people here?" It made a creepy feeling go up her spine to think of some unseen inhabitant of the island who might possibly be spying on her at this moment from behind the big trees. "I never did quite like this island," she thought, "even on the Fourth of July."

Still, the island seemed better than the river, and what concerned her now was that most of the berries had been eaten.

"I had better go back for a pail and save what I can to share with Andy," she thought. But just as she started to turn back a flutter of white at the far side of the clearing caught her eye. She left Dot picking berries and stuffing them into her mouth, while she moved cautiously forward.

What she saw at the far side of the clearing surprised her. It was not at all what she had expected. Three white hens, their feathers damp and bedraggled as if they had been in the flood, were scratching and pecking in the moss and leaves under the trees. They seemed quite at home, clucking and ruffling their feathers as if they were in their own barnyard.

Sparrow was about to call, "Chick! chick! chick!" to them, because where there are hens there are bound to be eggs. But before she had made a sound she saw something else which made her heart begin to pound. A sleek red fox was creeping through the grass and ferns, stalking the chickens. He was so intent upon catching one that he did not even notice Sparrow. And the hens were as unconscious of the fox as the fox was of Sparrow.

In another moment the fox would have pounced on the nearest hen and dragged her off for his dinner. But Sparrow would not allow that.

"Hey!" she cried. "You get out of here, you fox! You leave those hens alone, do you hear?"

The fox heard. Away he ran, like a red streak, and disappeared into the woods. The hens, suddenly alerted to danger, began to squawk and flop about in terror.

"Oh, hens," Sparrow said, "we need you more than the fox does. I've got to get you." But a night on the river in a broken coop, a shipwreck on an island, and an adventure with a fox all combined to put the hens in a nervous state. The harder Sparrow tried to catch them, the faster they ran. It was useless to chase them. Sparrow stopped and began to coax them. "Dear hens," she wheedled, "I've just saved your lives. What more do you want? You might be grateful enough to come and lay eggs for us."

Something about her coaxing voice reminded the chickens of safe barnyards and scattered corn. They stopped and looked at her, but they would not let her catch them. Finally Sparrow remembered the half-eaten sandwich in her pocket. She would have liked to eat it herself, but now she took it out of the paper and began to break off crumbs and toss them toward the hens. Gradually the hens drew nearer and began to pick up crumbs.

"If I can only lure them down to our camp, Andy will know how to catch them," Sparrow thought. Everything seemed to be going beautifully, and Sparrow hoped that she could make the bits of sandwich last until she could lure the hens down to the shore. But suddenly Tiddley came back from chasing a squirrel. He felt very pleased with himself, and now, when he saw chickens, he dashed away after them, barking joyously. The three hens scattered in three directions and disappeared into the woods.

"Oh, Tiddley, you wicked dog!" cried Sparrow. Tiddley came wagging up to her, expecting praise, and he looked disappointed to get a scolding instead. "We might as well go back," Sparrow said sadly. "There's no use trying to find the hens now. Maybe we can get them later. And it's hardly worth while to come back with a bucket to pick berries, there are so few left. I wonder who picked them, I just wonder!"

Dot had managed to find enough berries to make her mouth and cheeks all blue, and she did not want to go back to the shore. But Sparrow picked her up and carried her, squalling and kicking, down the hill. Campbell and Tiddley followed along behind. Sparrow's spirits were very low, and when she heard a great outcry from the camp they sank lower still.

"What next?" she said. "Surely things can't get any worse!"

"Who's on This Island?"

As she went down the hill, Sparrow could hear Lily Belle's voice crying, "Help! help! help!" Lily Belle had cried, "Help!" so often that, as with the boy in the old tale who cried, "Wolf! Wolf!" nobody paid much attention to her. But this time Sparrow heard Andy shouting too, and he sounded excited.

A faint trace of smoke spiraled in the air, and Sparrow thought, "Lily Belle must have got fire, and they're shouting for joy because we can have a campfire."

Tiddley ran ahead, barking, and Sparrow went as fast as she could with Dot in her arms. But the nearer she came to the camp, the less joyful the shouting sounded. The

first thing Sparrow saw when she came through the trees
to the beach was a cloud of smoke, and in the midst of it
sat Lily Belle, still rubbing blazing sticks together and
shouting, "Help!" The beautiful blue apron which Sparrow
had given her blazed merrily; even her blue hair ribbon
was on fire. Andy and Bucket were running toward the
river to get water.

"Oh, dear!" Sparrow cried. "I never should have left
her rubbing sticks together. She couldn't know what to
do with fire when she got it, and now she's burning up!"
She set Dot down and began to run toward the burning
robot. "Oh, Lily Belle! Dear Lily Belle!" she wailed.

Lily Belle jumped up and began to dance about now in a
way which threatened to break all her records, and still
she shouted, "Help!"

"We're coming, Lily Belle," Andy cried. "Hurry,
Bucket, get water! Put out fire!"

Bucket filled his pails at the river's edge and came
running. He emptied both pails over Lily Belle's head.
The hot tin sizzled, the flame went out, and Lily Belle
gurgled sadly, "Ho—Ho—Ho—" She had a very large
hole in the middle of her apron, her hair ribbon had gone
up in smoke, and one of her tin curls had come unsoldered.
Her face was black with soot. She looked a pathetic sight.

They all stood and gazed at her. Supercan with his ax
beside him, Bucket with his pails still dripping, and little
Campbell with Sparrow's hanky pressed to his cheek

looked without any show of emotion. But Andy and Sparrow could not help showing sorrow and distress in their faces. Even Tiddley drooped his tail. For a moment no one spoke. Then Dot came toddling up to them. As they already knew, Dot had an odd sense of humor for a baby, and now she said, "Poor 'ily Belle!" and burst out laughing. She pointed at the robot and laughed, and suddenly Andy and Sparrow began to laugh too. Lily Belle was a mess, but she did look funny when you stopped to think about it. In a moment her run-down "ho—ho—ho—"'s turned into merry "ha-ha-ha"s, and she began laughing too.

"We might as well be joyful," Andy said between bursts of laughter. At the word "joyful," the other three robots, who were learning fast, began to caper and dance as Sparrow had taught them to do.

"Well!" Sparrow said at last. "Anybody would think we had something to be pleased about. We really haven't, you know. Where in the world are we going to get a new apron to make Lily Belle decent?"

"Haven't you got an extra petticoat or something?" Andy asked.

"But Lily Belle's so much bigger around the waist than I am," Sparrow objected. "My apron only fit her because it had long strings."

"That's a girls' problem," Andy said. "I don't care what she wears. But the really wonderful thing is that she got fire. She really did, and now we've gone and put it out.

We need a campfire. Now we'll have to start all over again. Lily Belle, will you try again?"

"I shouldn't think she'd want to try again," Sparrow said. "Just look at the poor thing."

"But next time we would watch her and tell her what to do to get the campfire started instead of burning herself up."

"Well, first I'm going to tidy her," Sparrow said. "The campfire will just have to wait a little while."

Sparrow took Lily Belle down to the river and washed her face and hands and polished up her tin. Then she took off her own petticoat, split it up the back, and knotted the unburned apron strings to the waistband on each side so that it made a fairly good substitute for an apron. The apron was white instead of blue, but otherwise Lily Belle looked as good as new. Of course one curl was still missing.

"Now, dear," Sparrow said, "I'm afraid your curl is gone because we do not have any solder to stick it back with, but you're clean and neat again, and I'll put a flower in your hair instead of the hair ribbon, and all the other curls are in place, and you look as much like a girl again as I can make you."

"What if she burns herself up again, rubbing sticks?" Andy asked. "You might have waited a while to clean her up."

"I'll watch her this time," Sparrow said.

"We'll both watch her," said Andy. "Then we'll be extra sure."

So they set Lily Belle to rubbing sticks together once more, and this time both Andy and Sparrow sat beside her to see that she came to no harm.

While Lily Belle was rubbing her sticks, Andy pointed out the improvements he had been making in the campsite. Inside a safe ring of stones he had piled dry twigs for the campfire. Just beyond were fragrant mounds of balsam boughs for beds, and over these was a half-built shelter of green saplings and branches.

"My! Andy, you've done a lot!" said Sparrow.

"It's pretty good, isn't it?" said Andy proudly. "Go on, Supercan and Bucket, finish the wickiup now, like good robots."

"Can they do it themselves?" Sparrow marveled.

"Once you teach them what to do, they go right on doing it." Andy felt well satisfied with his robots and his camp, and most of all with himself. "I'm a very inventive boy," he added, as modestly as he could.

At Andy's command the large tin men had set to work with their usual strength and energy. Supercan would chop down several saplings; then he and Bucket would seize the fallen poles and rush with them to the wickiup, where they would stick them into the ground and bend the tops together to form a shelter. It was marvelous to watch them.

Tiddley was delighted with all this activity. He did not understand the tin men at all. Every time he tried to nip one of their heels, he hurt his teeth, but he enjoyed racing after them as they worked. Dot and Campbell, with "b'anky" and hanky pressed to their cheeks, stood contentedly watching.

Suddenly Andy remembered something. "What about food, Sparrow? Did you find anything? I'm getting hungry."

Sparrow was ashamed that she had not had better luck while Andy had been doing all these wonderful things.

"We found some berries," she said.

"So I see by Dot's face. You might have washed *her*, when you washed Lily Belle. Cousin Eva would probably be shocked." Dot looked at him with a wide grin on her dirty face. She seemed to be enjoying herself as much as he was.

"Oh, Andy," Sparrow said, "I have a lot to tell you, but all this excitement with Lily Belle drove it out of my head. We might even have eggs to boil, if we could catch the hens."

"Hens?" cried Andy in surprise.

"Yes, they are probably hens from your own farm, Andy. I think the flood must have washed them down here. There are all sorts of animals on this island. I could hear them rustling all around in the ferns and bushes, and I saw a fox. He was just about to catch one of the hens when I scared him away."

"Great frogs and catfish!" Andy cried. "We'd better get those hens before the fox does! What else have you got to tell?"

"Well, Andy, there's someone else on this island besides ourselves. I'm sure of it."

"Did you see anyone?"

"No, but the berry bushes were all trampled in one place, and the berries had been picked. It was kind of scary."

"Hmm," Andy said, thinking hard. "You didn't see any boats or people or anything?"

"No, just hens, and I tried to lure them down here with sandwich crumbs, because I knew you would want them. But then Tiddley ran up barking, and the hens ran away into the woods."

"HELP!" shouted Lily Belle. She had fire again! This time Andy and Sparrow managed to get the blazing sticks away from her and under the dry twigs in time to start the campfire. Soon it was blazing away very pleasantly.

Andy was so happy that he almost forgot about the hens and the mysterious berrypicker. "Now we're *really* camping, when we get a campfire going!" he cried. "Keep putting on twigs, Sparrow, and I'll fill one of Bucket's pails and put it on to boil. We'll have safe water to drink, even if we don't have food."

"Remember the hens, Andy," Sparrow said as she hastened to put fuel on the fire. "If you can catch them, we might have boiled eggs."

"That's right," Andy said. "I'll go after them in just a few minutes. If they are from our farm, it ought to be easy to get them. Goodness knows, I've done enough for those hens in my life. They ought to be grateful enough to lay us some eggs."

While Andy and Sparrow were busy building up the campfire and putting a pail of water on to boil, Supercan and Bucket kept right on working. They kept cutting saplings and dragging them along and setting them up against the side of the wickiup until it began to grow very large. Tiddley still ran at their heels, snapping and barking and making a nuisance of himself. Just as they were about to lean a couple more saplings against the tottering pile, Tiddley ran between the tin men and caught Supercan by the ankle. Supercan fell forward against Bucket. Bucket fell against the overloaded shelter. There was a clatter of cans, a ringing of Supercan's bell, and the whole shelter crashed over in a pile of leaves and branches and tin arms and legs.

"Oh, my wickiup!" cried Andy. "There goes my wickiup."

Sparrow looked around nervously, and she could not help saying, "Wickiwhat?"

"My wickiup!" wailed Andy.

"Oh, dear!" cried Sparrow. "It looks like a wickidown to me."

Well, there are lots of trials in camping. It is not all lemon meringue pie and banana splits. Andy was finding that out. Now he had to set the robots on their feet, and pull the saplings out of the pile, and tie Tiddley up with a long piece of grapevine, and start all over to build the

wickiup. Sparrow helped as much as she could, but she began to feel more and more depressed about the whole situation.

"Look, Andy," she said, "why don't you just try to mend the boat and get away from here? I never did like this island, even on the Fourth of July, and I don't want to stay until snow flies, honestly I don't."

"Everything's going to be all right, Sparrow," said Andy

patiently. "As soon as I get the wickiup up again, I'll go looking for the hens, and we'll have some nice boiled eggs and blackberries, and we'll really be camping. You'll like it then, Sparrow."

"I hope so," Sparrow said. She did not feel sure.

So, as soon as the wickiup was properly built, Andy started off to catch the hens. "It will only be a few minutes," he said. "The hens will know me, I'm sure."

135

But Andy did not realize how frightened the hens were. The flood, the strange island, the fox, even Sparrow and Tiddley had frightened them more than they had ever been frightened in their lives. The slightest noise set them to running away through the grass and ferns. Once or twice Andy caught glimpses of them, scurrying through the underbrush or flying into low branches ahead of him. But they would not come near him, and certainly they were not going to let him catch them.

He went by the berry patch and picked a few berries, but he saw what Sparrow meant by the trodden-down place where some other picker had been.

"Yoohoo!" he called. "Who's on this island? Come out, whoever you are!"

But the only answer that he got was an echo of his own voice.

"Yoohoo-whoever-you-are."

When he returned to camp with no hens and no eggs and a rather scared look on his face, Sparrow said, "Oh, Andy, I want to go home."

That was almost the last straw.

Bucket Is Missing

As Andy said, it did no good to want to go home. "How can we?" he asked. "We have to do the best we can here for now, Sparrow."

"I know," Sparrow said. "But Andy, I do think that you might try to mend the boat before you spend so much time making a camp where we can stay until snow flies."

"It's a good camp," Andy said, looking around proudly.

"Yes, it is. But please look at the boat now. How can we ever get home if we don't mend the boat?"

"Okay," Andy said, "whether we eat or sleep, or not, I guess we've got to mend the boat."

"You've been putting it off all summer, Andy," Sparrow said, "and now it's needed more than ever before."

"Okay," Andy said again.

They went to the water's edge and looked at the boat. The hole in the bottom of it was large and jagged. It would take a big patch to mend it.

"Supercan, help me turn the boat over," Andy ordered. Supercan stepped up smartly, and together he and Andy hoisted the boat on its side and turned it over. They all gathered around and looked again at the hole in the over-turned boat, and they did not feel very cheerful about it. No one could ever say again that it would leak a little, small amount.

"Oh, that boat!" Andy groaned. All summer long it had been a reproach to him, and now the sight of it really made him angry. He went up and gave it a kick. "I'd like to knock the old thing to pieces. Bam! Bam! Bam!"

As soon as Andy had spoken, up came Supercan with the ax, and he was just about to start knocking the boat to pieces when Andy stopped him.

"No, no, no! Don't do it, Supercan!" cried Andy, already ashamed of his temper. "Honest, I didn't mean what I said. We must save the boat if we can."

"The robots don't understand being angry any more than they understand being joyful, Andy," said Sparrow reasonably. "You have to remember that and set a good example for them."

Andy did not feel like setting a good example for any-one at that moment, but he saw that nothing else could be done.

"All right," he said. "Supercan, you and I will try to split and shape a new floor board to fit the hole in the boat. And Bucket will have to go out and find enough pitch to make it stick in place. Sparrow, you'll have to go with Bucket and show him how to scrape the pitch off the pine trees and collect it in one of the pails."

"Me?" said Sparrow in a small voice. "Must I go up in this island again?"

"I'd be glad to go," Andy said, "but can you cut and shape a board to fit the hole in the boat while I'm gone?"

"No-o, I can't," Sparrow said.

"Then I'll do that first, and afterward I'll go and show Bucket how to collect pitch. It will take longer that way, of course."

Sparrow thought this over. "I'll go," she said at last.

"You'll be perfectly safe, Sparrow," Andy said. "With Bucket beside you, nothing will touch you. Remember how scared the animals all used to be until they got used to him? Remember how scared you were yourself the first time you saw him?"

"I remember," Sparrow said. "But before I go, Andy, I'll have to do something with Dot and Campbell. I can't drag them along all over the island."

"The wickiup is all right now," Andy said. "You can put Dot to sleep in it."

"You're sure it's safe?"

"Safe as a house."

"But will she like it?"

Dot was watching them with round blue eyes. She was clutching her "b'anky" and sucking her thumb, but she seemed to be in an unusually pleasant frame of mind. Sparrow spread her raincoat on the balsam bed in the wickiup and invited Dot to lie down. To their surprise Dot came and lay down without a single "no."

"I think she likes to camp," Andy said. "It's the first time that we have both liked the same thing at the same time. She's really quite a nice baby after all."

"Maybe she was bored at home," suggested Sparrow. "Maybe she just wanted some adventures."

"Well, we can sure give them to her!" said Andy. "But now she'd better get some rest."

"Campbell will sit on one side of Dottie, and Lily Belle will sit on the other side and sing, and Dottie will take a nice long nap," coaxed Sparrow.

"Take my raincoat to cover her," Andy said. "It's too bad we don't have the pink pajamas with the bunnies on them, but this way she will learn to rough it. Anyway, she's got her old rag of a blanket."

"B'anky," corrected Dot sleepily. She put her thumb back in her mouth, and Lily Belle began to sing. In a moment Dot had gone to sleep. She did look like a lovely baby when she was asleep.

"I'd like to go to sleep too," Sparrow said. "I didn't sleep a wink all night."

"Neither did I," said Andy. "But if I can keep going, I guess you can too." Andy had already started to show Supercan the right tree to fell to get the right piece of wood to shape into a patch for the boat.

Sparrow sighed. Then she looked around for Bucket. "Here, Bucket, you and I have work to do. Come along now."

Bucket stepped up obediently and waited for further instructions.

"You know how the pitch oozes out of the pine trees, Sparrow," Andy called. "Now what you have to do is to find some nice pitchy pine trees and show Bucket how to scrape the stuff off into one of his pails. He'll soon get the knack of it and all you'll have to do is to go along and see that he keeps out of trouble."

"All right," Sparrow said. She tried to sound as brave as she could. She led the way up toward the center of the island with Bucket crashing along behind her. He did not bother to walk around a bush or a clump of fern but plunged right through it with a great deal of noise. The birds flew up, scolding and screaming; the squirrels and small island animals fled in all directions, squeaking and chattering.

At the first pine tree Sparrow stopped and looked for pitch. She could see small glassy drops of it oozing out of the side of the tree. She took a sharp stick and tried to show Bucket how to use it to scrape the pitch into his pail. But, having only a hook where his hand should have been, Bucket could not hold the stick. It looked as if Sparrow would have to do the scraping herself, but she could not reach as high up the tree as Bucket could, and that made another difficulty. Sparrow began to feel that this was as hopeless a task as looking for food. She grew more and more discouraged.

Fortunately robots do not become discouraged. When

Bucket finally understood what was wanted, he threw away the stick and began to scrape the pitch with his hook. This worked very well, and the robot did not seem to mind how pitchy and sticky he became. The work went slowly, for only about half of the pitch got into the pail. But Bucket seemed to enjoy his work, and he crashed from tree to tree with cheerful industry.

All Sparrow needed to do now was to follow him and see that he kept at work. She had time to think her own thoughts at last, and they were not very gay ones. Up to this time she had been too busy to remember how hungry and tired she was, and that she had lost her home and dear Grandpa Clayton. Now she remembered that yesterday at this time she had been cooking a nice fish dinner for Grandpa Clayton in their cozy home, and that he had come in smiling to help her eat it.

"The river is rising fast, Sparrow," he had said. "But we're on high ground here. I think we'll be safe."

But they had not been safe at all. The river had kept on rising, and Mr. and Mrs. Buckram were gone too. As she thought of all these things, Sparrow's troubles overwhelmed her and she began to cry. "Even if we melt pitch and get the right-sized board to patch the boat, it may not stick; and I don't want to stay on this island until the snow flies, no matter how fine a camp Andy makes. I don't! I don't!"

Sparrow kept stumbling along after Bucket, but the more she thought about her troubles, the harder she cried. She had given her hanky to Campbell for a "b'anky," and she had only the backs of her hands to wipe away her tears. The trees began to blur and run together and the roots and bushes to catch at her feet. Presently she gave up trying to be brave and sat down on a log to have her cry.

"Oh, dear! Oh, dear!" Sparrow sobbed, covering her face with her hands. She could hear Bucket crashing on through the underbrush, but for the moment she did not care. He could do very well by himself, and she would soon catch up with him. Now she could only sit there and cry, hoping to feel better soon.

And in fact, her sobs gradually grew less. Finally she gave a long sigh and remembered that she had a stick of Doublemint gum in her pocket. She had been saving it for a bad moment, and this certainly was one. She drew the stick out of her pocket and broke it in half. She put one half in her mouth. The other half she wrapped and put back in her pocket, for she knew that there might always be another emergency.

The Doublemint flavor spread pleasantly along her tongue and all through her mouth. It was very comforting. She gave one last sob and wiped her eyes on her sleeve. The trees and bushes no longer blurred and ran together when she looked at them. The woods seemed very quiet now, but she did notice a little rustling noise nearby. Sparrow turned her head to look. Standing among the ferns and staring out at her was a small pink pig. In a moment she had forgotten all her troubles. "Pigs!" she cried. "My goodness, we've got everything!"

At the sound of her voice, the pig uttered a nervous squeal and ran away into the woods. "It must be a Buckram pig," Sparrow said to herself. "They always were a nervous lot. The cows and the chickens soon got used to the robots, but the pigs never did. This pig couldn't have seen Bucket or he would never have come so near. *Bucket!* Where is he?"

Now she realized for the first time that she could no longer hear the tin man crashing through the brush. Even the birds had settled down in the silent woods, and the squirrels and field mice had resumed their quiet scurryings. Bucket had completely disappeared.

Sparrow started forward in alarm and began to call, "Bucket! Bucket! Where are you? Come here! Come here!" But only her own voice echoed back to her. She could hear the pig running through the brush, but from Bucket not the slightest sound could be heard.

"Oh, now I *am* in trouble," cried Sparrow. "What will Andy say if I have lost his robot?" She ran here and there among the trees, looking and calling, "Bucket! Bucket!" But she might as well have saved her breath. There was no sign of the robot anywhere.

Finally there seemed nothing left to do but to go back and tell Andy what had happened and get him to help her. As she ran down the hill past the berry patch, something suddenly made her pause. In the soft ground she could see the tracks made by herself and Dot and Tiddley earlier in the day, and she could also see a lot of muddled tracks left by the mysterious berrypicker. One or two of these were very clear, and she stopped to examine them. They were large, but the person must have been barefoot, for these were certainly not shoe tracks. The impressions were quite fresh and must have been made since she had been here before. As Sparrow looked, the hair began to prickle on the top of her head. The tracks were, indeed, something like a large bare foot, but, instead of toes, the marks at the end were sharp and narrow as if they had been made by claws!

"A bear!" Sparrow said to herself. "Bears love berries too, I know they do! There must be a great big bear on this very island with us. Oh, Andy!"

Sparrow was too breathless when she first reached the camp to speak. Andy and Supercan were busily shaping and cutting down a board to fit the hole in the boat. Dot was still sleeping, and Lily Belle and Campbell were sitting cozily beside the fire. It all looked very nice and peaceful, and Sparrow did not know how to break her bad news.

Andy looked up and said, "Well, did you get the pitch? We're nearly ready for it."

"He's gone," Sparrow blurted.

"Who?"

"Bucket. I've lost him."

"No!"

"Yes, it's true, and he's got the pitch. And, oh, Andy, there's a bear on this island, and I think—I think it must be awfully big."

"Great frogs and catfish!" For a moment Andy could not think of any other words to say.

Lost and Found

Once a robot is told to do something, he goes right ahead doing it until somebody stops him. When Sparrow sat down on the fallen log to have her cry, Bucket kept on going from pine tree to pine tree to scrape off the pitch. He walked through the ferns and bushes and stumbled over the logs, but nothing stopped him.

He went over the hump of the island, and on the other side he fell into a hole with a great clatter of tin. But presently he got himself untangled and out of the hole, and he went on again as if nothing had happened. A little way down the other slope he came upon the fox stalking the hens.

Bucket went right on scraping pitch off the pine trees into his bucket and paying no attention to the fox or the chickens. But the fox was nearly frightened out of its wits by the sight of the tin man. It darted away, leaving the chickens to flop and squawk in terror at their narrow escape.

However, the terror of the hens lasted only a few moments. They looked up from their flopping and squawking, and there was Bucket calmly scraping pitch off the pine trees. The hens had not recognized Andy or Sparrow, but even the most stupid hen could not fail to recognize Bucket. Bucket had brought them food and water at their happy home on the Buckram farm! With clucks and cacklings of delight the three hens flew at the tin man. One landed on his head, one on his shoulder, and the third one sat down in the pail and laid an egg on top of the pitch.

Now, with three hens riding along, Bucket found it hard to continue collecting pitch. But because there was no one there to tell him to stop, he kept on going through brush and over logs. The three hens jogged along with him, happy to be carried by someone they trusted.

When Bucket reached the other side of the island, he started to walk off into the river, but then he noticed that the pine trees were all behind him. He had been sent out to collect pitch from the pine trees, and that was what he would do until somebody stopped him. So he turned around, just as the water began to lap about his feet, and walked back across the island toward the pine trees.

In the meantime Andy and Supercan had started off to find Bucket or the bear or whatever came first.

"Sparrow, you stay here this time," Andy said. "Dot is likely to wake up now, and she's sure to be cross and hungry. Keep the campfire burning so we can melt the pitch if we ever find Bucket. Lily Belle and Campbell will keep you company."

"Oh, Andy, be careful," Sparrow begged. "We've all got to stay together as well as we can."

"Everything will be all right," Andy said. He was trying to be as cheerful as he could. "Don't worry about a thing. Come on, Supercan."

Supercan's little bell went dingling and dongling merrily through the woods as he walked. "I hope Bucket will hear it," Andy thought. "Maybe it will make him want to come back. Surely he can't be very far away."

Every few moments Andy shouted, "Yoohoo! Yoohoo! Bucket, come back!" But the only reply he got was an echo of his own voice: "Bucket, come back!"

Andy went ahead of Supercan through the woods, but when they reached the berry patch he stopped to look for bear tracks and to listen. Supercan stopped too, and the woods were very still for a few moments. Andy had just discovered the tracks which had frightened Sparrow, and he was leaning over to examine them, when he heard a sound of scuffling and sniffling at the other side of the patch. "There's something over there," he said. "Come on, Supercan."

Now there was a sound of growling and a sound of squealing. As Andy ran through the berry bushes he could see that some kind of struggle was going on nearby. Suddenly a very large black bear reared up on his hind legs in front of him. In his paws, hugged to his breast, was one of the Buckrams' pigs. The pig squealed and kicked, but the bear held him tight.

Andy gave a shout, and the bear turned around and saw him. Andy stopped running, and he and the bear looked at each other. To Andy the bear on his hind legs looked very large, and suddenly Andy felt very small. The bear growled and showed his teeth, and now he began to come toward Andy.

For a few seconds Andy stood still. But the nearer the bear came, the better it seemed to him to start running in the opposite direction. And that is what he did. He turned around and ran as fast as he could away from the bear.

Supercan, however, kept on going forward, his little bell ringing, his bulb eyes gleaming. He walked slowly and steadily straight at the bear.

Suddenly the bear dropped the pig, went down on all fours, and lumbered away into the woods. Soon he was running as fast as Andy was, but in the opposite direction. As for Supercan, he went calmly ahead as if nothing had happened. He crashed through the ferns and bushes, and his bell rang.

Andy did not stop running for some time. When he finally grew a little calmer and saw that the bear was not

following him, he sat down to catch his breath and find out where he was. The part of the island where he found himself was entirely strange to him, and Supercan was nowhere to be seen. He could not even hear the ringing of Supercan's bell. Now he began to shout, "Supercan! Bucket! Where are you? Come back, Supercan! Come back, Bucket!" But the only reply he got was an echo: "Come back! Come back!"

Supercan went striding straight across the island, but he was puzzled and confused because he did not know what he was supposed to be doing. Andy had given him no particular command. He had simply told him to come along, and Supercan understood that they were hunting for something. It could not be the bear, because when Andy saw the bear he ran away from it. So they must be hunting for something else. If Andy had clearly said, "Find Bucket," Supercan would undoubtedly have gone straight to the spot where Bucket could be found. But Andy had said, "Come along, Supercan." Supercan was not sure if he was to pick berries or look for Bucket or scare bears. Now that Andy had disappeared in the opposite direction from the bear, Supercan kept on going in his own direction. *Dingle, dingle, dong,* rang his little bell. It sounded like a cowbell ringing in the woods.

The pig that had been rescued from the bear began to follow Supercan. He had now begun to feel that the robot was his friend, and certainly his recent experience had taught him that bears were more terrible than tin men.

Soon three pigs were following Supercan and hoping that he would lead them back to their happy home at the Buckram farm.

Supercan paid no attention to them but continued on to the other side of the island. The ringing of his bell frightened away the wild creatures, but it was a very comforting sound to the domestic animals that had been lost in the flood.

Daisy, the cow, who had spent an unpleasant night swimming in the river and had been half drowned by the time she reached land, was now eating grass at the far side of the island. When she heard a familiar bell, she raised her head and gave a long *moo-oo-oo*. She had found plenty to eat, but she wanted very much to be milked and properly cared for.

The little bell came nearer and nearer, and Daisy left her eating and began to trot toward it. This was the best sound she had heard in a long time. She was so glad to see Supercan that she almost knocked him over trying to rub her horns against him.

Supercan, who had been puzzled to know what he was supposed to do, now felt better. He had been sent out to find something, and here was something that he had found. He took hold of the piece of rope that still hung to Daisy's halter and began to lead her back across the island to Andy's camp.

Robots Return

As Andy had predicted, Dot awoke in a very cross and hungry mood.

"Din-din!" she cried. "Dottie wa din-din."

Sparrow was so hungry herself that she understood perfectly what Dot wanted. "Dinner will come, Dottie," Sparrow said, hoping very much that she was not fibbing. "Here's a blackberry. Eat a nice, nice blackberry, baby." Dot opened her mouth and accepted the berry. It was sweet and good, and she would have been glad to make a meal of berries, but Sparrow had only two more. These were all she could find in scouting about the camp.

When Dot had finished them, she took Sparrow's hand

and started up the trail toward the berry patch. But Sparrow knew that she must stay at the camp until Andy returned, if they were to remain together at all and not become hopelessly lost on this strange island.

"No, Dottie, no," Sparrow said. "We must wait until Andy comes back with Supercan and Bucket." Now Dot's mouth began to turn down at the corners, and her eyes squinched shut. Two big tears oozed out under the closed eyelids, the mouth began to open wider, and finally out came a wonderful roar of grief and anger. Tiddley was very much worried. He ran up, barking and whining and trying to lick Dot's hand. Dot only kicked her heels and roared. Campbell offered her his hanky, and Lily Belle began to sing. But nothing would please her.

When Andy, tired and hungry, arrived back at camp without the robots, the first thing he heard was Dot's roaring. By this time Lily Belle was yelling, "Help!" and Tiddley was howling, and, yes, it's true, Sparrow was sobbing, "Dear, oh, dear!"

Campbell came and held up his arms to Andy, and Andy was so pleased that Campbell was not howling or screaming or roaring or sobbing that he took him up and kissed him on the nose.

"There, Campbell," he said, "and you might as well know I'll never do it again, so don't come begging. But I sure am glad that I didn't give you any kind of noise-maker. You're the most sensible person here right now, and I'll be proud to shake your hand."

At this Campbell stood up very straight and proud and offered Andy his hand. He looked more like a small man than a baby, Andy thought, and Andy patted him on the head and shook his hand.

"Oh, Andy," Sparrow sobbed, "I hope you found the robots and brought us something to eat. We're not very cheerful here."

"So I see—or rather hear," said Andy. "Do you want me to howl too?"

"No," said Sparrow, drying her eyes on her sleeve. "We've howled enough." Andy slapped Lily Belle on the back, and the cries for help stopped. That was something. Now Tiddley stopped howling and came up to Andy hopefully, wagging his tail.

When everyone else had stopped making a noise, Dot stopped too and looked around in surprise. There was a wonderful sweet silence, and then Andy said, "I'm sorry, Sparrow, I haven't brought anything back. I saw the bear and I ran, and now Supercan is gone too. I've lost both robots, and the boat isn't mended, and I'm hungry, and if I had some fishline and hooks I could fish, but I don't have any, and Mother and Daddy and your grandpa are gone in the flood, and, I must say, everything looks pretty dark and gloomy."

Sparrow saw that Andy was just where she had been earlier in the day. She took the half-stick of Doublemint gum out of her pocket and broke it in half again. "Here, Andy," she said, "chew this. It's small, but it will help."

"Thank you," Andy said, putting the small piece of gum into his mouth. It was very comforting.

"And Andy," Sparrow went on, "at least it isn't raining. The river isn't getting any higher. And you are so good at inventions, can't you invent a fishtrap or something?"

"Well, as you said, it's hard to invent things without tin and solder and pieces and parts," Andy said. "We don't even have any rope or string. But maybe I could make a fishtrap out of willow twigs and pieces of grapevine. I'll try. But it will be some time before we're likely to catch a fish."

"I'll help you," Sparrow said. "There ought to be willows growing at the water's edge, and I saw wild grapevines up in the woods."

But before they had found the first grapevine or a suitable willow tree they heard a crashing sound in the underbrush above them. It sounded as if someone was walking straight along through bushes and ferns without trying to find a path.

"If it's the bear," cried Sparrow, "what shall we do?"

"We'll be brave," Andy said. "This time I won't run."

"And I won't cry."

Still, it was not very pleasant to hear that crashing sound, coming nearer and nearer. Standing close together, they looked up into the dark woods and waited. And suddenly, instead of a bear or some other frightening thing, there came Bucket! He was marching along with a hen on either shoulder and one on top of his head.

"Bucket!" they cried. "Good Bucket!"

He came down by the fire and held out his pail to Andy. It was half full of dried pitch, and resting neatly on top of the pitch were three very fresh eggs.

"Eggs!" cried the children. "Food!"

The other bucket had been on the campfire all this time, and the water in it was boiling merrily. It took Sparrow only a moment to pop the eggs into the boiling water. There was an egg for Dot, an egg for Andy, and an egg for Sparrow.

"Thank goodness the robots don't eat," Sparrow said. "And I'll give Tiddley a part of mine." When the eggs were cooked, she used the cups from the Thermos bottles to fish them out of the boiling water. It was hard to wait until they were cool enough to open and eat, and Dot kept saying, "Din-din," and stretching out her hands.

"Just a little, small minute," said Sparrow. "We haven't any spoons, so we've got to let the eggs cool enough for fingers."

While Sparrow was cooking the eggs, Andy had set the pail of pitch to melt at the edge of the campfire.

"Bucket, you are a hero!" Andy said. "You are a good, good robot. I am very pleased, and I wish I had a medal for you."

Bucket sat down by the fire, and his face looked as stern as ever, but his light-bulb eyes sparkled with something like pleasure or satisfaction.

At this moment there sounded a dinging and a donging like a little cowbell in the woods.

"Supercan!" cried Andy. "He's coming back too!" There was an even greater crashing sound than Bucket had made. It sounded as if two robots were coming instead of one.

"Maybe he's bringing the bear," Sparrow said. But with an egg to eat, she was not very worried any more.

Andy and Sparrow both began to run toward the sound,

shouting, "Supercan! Supercan!" Then they saw the cow, and their shouts turned to cries of "Daisy! Daisy!"

"Great frogs and catfish!" Andy cried. "Now we've got milk!"

It was an exciting moment of reunion for everyone. Daisy was as pleased to see Andy as Andy was pleased to see her. Andy emptied the boiling water out of the egg pail so that it could be used for milk. While Sparrow fed Daisy choice bits of grass and clover, Andy sat down and milked the cow. By the time the eggs were cool enough to handle, Andy had a pail full of warm, foaming milk to go with them.

This was the best meal that Andy and Sparrow had ever eaten, and Dot enjoyed it without a single "No!" When the children had drunk all the milk they wanted, and filled the two Thermos bottles, they allowed Tiddley to finish off the remainder. With his head in the pail and his tail wagging, he was as happy as they were.

The robots stood around watching these strange proceedings with interest. They did not know at all why food should be so important to people who were not made out of tin. When Andy looked up and saw them watching him, he remembered all that the robots had done for him.

"Supercan and Bucket, you are wonderful," he said. "We never could have come through this flood without you. I wish I had a medal for each of you."

"And don't forget Lily Belle," said Sparrow. "It was Lily Belle who got fire for us."

"Yes, I'd give Lily Belle a medal too, if I had one. But first of all, now I've got to mend the boat."

After his satisfying meal, Andy was quite ready to go to work. He fitted the new board onto the bottom of the boat and poured the melted pitch around it and into all the leaky cracks. It looked like a pretty good job.

"How soon can we try it?" Sparrow asked.

"Not until tomorrow," said Andy. "The pitch has to cool and harden before it will do any good. And look how low the sun is getting. We'll have to spend the night here on the island."

"Oh, dear!" said Sparrow. "I don't like that idea at all. Sure you aren't saying that just because you want to camp out?"

"No, it's true," Andy said, "but it won't be bad. We've had a good meal, and we'll gather a lot of dry wood and keep the fire going all night. That will scare away wild animals and keep us warm, and if anybody is out on the river looking for survivors of the flood it will be a signal to them."

Court of Awards

While Sparrow was going along the shore, collecting drift-wood for the fire, she found other things which gave her ideas. Many odds and ends of wreckage had washed up with the driftwood. There was a broken chicken coop which would shelter the hens, and there was a cup without a handle which would certainly be useful. At present they had only two Thermos cups for three milk-drinkers. As she was washing out the cup, Sparrow noticed two small shiny things at the edge of the river. They twinkled so brightly in the setting sun that they reminded Sparrow of the robots' eyes, and at first she was disappointed to find out that they were only bottle caps. What could one do with a bottle cap? But when she found two more she began to think harder.

"They are small and round and absolutely useless without bottles," she thought. But Grandpa Clayton had taught her that nothing is really useless. "They look a little bit like medals," she said to herself. "Medals! Andy wanted medals to reward the robots. Why wouldn't bottle caps do? After all, the robots are made of cans. Why not make medals for them out of bottle caps?"

She put the four bottle caps in her pocket and ran back to Andy.

"Look, Andy," she said, "here are your medals." Andy was a very inventive boy, and he got the idea at once.

"Sure!" he said. "They'll make fine medals. We can stick them onto the robots' breasts with some of the pitch. We'll have a ceremony by the campfire as soon as it's dark. It will be something good to do before bedtime—something to keep us interested and cheerful. It can be a kind of court of awards. But you might as well throw one of the bottle caps away. We'll only need three."

"But Andy, there are four robots."

"I know," Andy said, "and I'm sorry for Campbell. But you know yourself, Sparrow, that a medal's no good if everybody has one. It has to be a reward for some good deed, or it's no medal at all. Supercan and Bucket have richly earned their medals, and, in a way, so has Lily Belle, but what has Campbell done?"

"He brought the ax," said Sparrow hopefully.

"I'm sorry," Andy said. "But if we gave Campbell a medal it would take all the glory out of the other three. You see that, don't you, Sparrow? I want to be fair, really I do."

"Yes," Sparrow said. "I expect you're right. But Campbell's so sweet."

"You just can't earn a medal by being sweet," said Andy patiently.

Sparrow understood this, but she did not throw the fourth bottle cap away. She put it back in her pocket beside the quarter of a stick of Doublemint gum, just in case one of the other medals should come unstuck or get lost. Another thing Grandpa Clayton had taught her was never to throw anything away. As soon as you did, it was sure to be needed.

When darkness came they were all quite happy and cheerful around the campfire. At Andy's direction the robots had rolled up two logs, one on either side of the fire. Andy and Sparrow and Dot settled themselves on one log, and the tin people sat in a row on the other one. The dancing firelight was reflected on the tin, so that it sparkled almost as brightly as their bulb eyes. They made a fine sight.

The hens had gone to roost in the broken coop; Tiddley was curled up asleep beside Sparrow and Dot; and Daisy was lying nearby, chewing her cud. Even the nervous pigs came near the fire, as if they knew that they were safer here than in the dark woods.

When everyone was quiet, Andy got up to make a speech.

"Tomorrow," Andy said, "I hope that we can make the boat work, and that we can reach a town where people will help us. Even if we had to stay on this island until snow flies, we wouldn't starve, now that we have hens and a cow." Here Sparrow shuddered, and Andy added hastily, "But I hope we won't have to stay here. So tonight everything looks much better than it did last night. I hope you all agree with me."

"Hear! hear!" said Sparrow. "Hooray!"

"Ray! ray!" said Dot, which surprised everyone, because she might just as well have said, "Ida wanna."

When Lily Belle heard that speeches were being made, she became very agitated. Her blue Christmas-tree-bulb eyes started to flash, and she began to roar, "My friends, now is the time to awaken to the dangers which surround us. The situation is very grave. Something must be done immediately—"

"No, no, Lily Belle," cried Sparrow, hastily jumping up to slap the robot on the back. "We're trying to forget the dangers which surround us tonight. Let Andy make the speeches."

Lily Belle subsided into silence, and Andy went on. "Now you robots have been very good and intelligent. I don't know how I ever happened to make you so well, nor how the lightning ever happened to electrify you so you would work without cords or batteries. I think if we get safely to land the scientists will want to study you, and probably there will be an article about you in *The Boy's Popular Mechanics Magazine*. But in the meantime, Sparrow and I would like you to know that we are very grateful to you for helping to save our lives. We are going to award some medals to the ones of you who have worked the hardest and done the most. It would be nice to give every one of you a medal, but, as you probably know, medals wouldn't mean very much if everybody had them. So tonight we are only going to award three medals, and we hope that anyone who is left out will not be disappointed."

The robots sat very quietly on their log, sparkling brightly in the firelight and giving Andy their most respectful attention. What they were waiting for, of course, was a command to do some kind of work. No one had told them to be joyful.

"Now," Andy said, "I will ask Supercan to step forward and receive his medal."

Supercan got up, with a clattering of tin and a jangling of his bell, and came to stand beside Andy.

"Supercan," Andy said, "for rowing the boat through darkness and flood and getting us safely to this island, for cutting down trees and shaping a board to mend the boat, and finally for bringing us a cow, I award you the First Class Medal for extraordinary merit."

Andy had polished up the bottle cap until it shone, and now he dipped the cork side of it into melted pitch and stuck it on Supercan's chest. It looked very impressive.

"Now stand over here, Supercan, and next I will ask
Bucket to come up and get his award." Bucket jumped up
so quickly that he nearly fell into the fire, but just in time
he saved himself and came to stand expectantly beside
Andy.

"Bucket," Andy said, "for bailing the boat which I hadn't got around to calking and painting before the rainy season started because at that time it only leaked a little, small amount, for collecting pitch to mend the boat, and for bringing us three hens and an equal number of eggs, I award you the Second Class Medal for extraordinary merit."

Bucket stood very straight and quiet while Andy stuck a shiny bottle cap on his chest. Then he took his place beside Supercan.

"Now, Lily Belle," Andy said, "I don't really approve of medals for girls, and you haven't done as much as Supercan and Bucket to deserve this honor, but come up here anyway." Lily Belle began to yodel as she took her place beside Andy, but Andy said, "Silence!" in a stern voice, and Lily Belle became silent.

"Lily Belle," Andy said, "for rubbing two sticks together and nearly burning yourself up to get this nice comfortable fire for us, I award you the Third Class Medal for—for merit."

"Don't forget that she kept us cheerful and that she took care of Dot and that she cried, 'Help,' at times when we needed help," reminded Sparrow.

"And times when we didn't need help too," said Andy. "But I'll change that to a Third Class Medal for *extraordinary* merit, if you like the sound of it better."

"I do," said Sparrow.

"All right, Lily Belle, here you are," said Andy as he

stuck the shiny bottle cap to her chest. "And now you may yodel if you want to. And I order all of you to be joyful. Be joyful, tin men and women, be joyful!"

Instantly the robots began to caper solemnly about. Even Campbell got off the log and began to caper, just as if he had received a medal himself.

"I wonder if he knows or cares," Sparrow thought. "Poor little Campbell! I love him even if he didn't earn a medal." She took Campbell's hand and began to teach the robots how to dance like Indians around a council fire.

Andy and Dot danced too, and Tiddley woke up and barked and ran around nipping at tin heels. The robots could have gone on dancing all night, but the human beings soon grew tired.

"We've had a hard day," Andy said at last. "Let's get some sleep, because tomorrow may be hard too. Stop dancing, tin men."

Andy piled up a heap of fuel beside the fire.

"Supercan," he said, "you are the fire-keeper. Every time that you have counted to five hundred, you must put a piece of wood on the fire. Do you understand?"

Supercan's little bell began to count: *Ding, ding, ding, ding. . . .* Before it had reached a hundred strokes, Sparrow and Dot were sound asleep on the balsam boughs in the wickiup. Andy stayed awake a little longer. He wanted to hear the five-hundredth *ding* and see if Supercan would remember what to do.

"Four hundred and ninety-eight," he counted, "four

hundred and ninety-nine, five hundred!" Then he heard
Supercan get up and put a piece of wood on the fire. In
the flickering light of the renewed flame he could see the
other robots sitting quietly on their log. As if Tiddley, too,
had been waiting for the reassuring fall of the log on the
fire, he came now and curled up against Andy's back.

"I guess it's all okey-dokey," Andy mumbled to himself.
He ceased to count the strokes of Supercan's bell, but the
monotonous sound of it lulled him very quickly into a deep
sleep.

The Fourth Bottle Cap

When Andy woke up in the morning, he was stiff and cold. The only warm spot on his body was the middle of his back, where Tiddley was still curled up asleep. For a moment Andy could not think where he was. He missed his comfortable bed and the walls of his small bedroom. "I'm out of doors!" he thought. "The sun is just coming up, the birds are singing. But what am I doing here?" Then he remembered the flood, and he sat up and looked around.

The fire was still burning low, and Supercan's bell was still counting five-hundreds. Through sleepy eyes Andy saw the robots sitting patiently on the log beside the fire. Daisy was cropping grass nearby, and the hens were beginning to flutter and cluck in the old coop. The pigs were rolling in the mud at the edge of the river. Tiddley uncurled himself and began to yawn and stretch.

Everything seemed to be as it had been the night before. Nearby Andy could see Sparrow curled up, sleeping with her coat pulled tight around her. She looked pale and tired, and he decided not to wake her until he had built the fire into a livelier blaze and had milked the cow.

He rubbed his eyes and shook himself and got up slowly. After he had dashed some water from the river onto his face and hands, Andy began to feel more like himself. He looked at the robots sitting patiently awaiting orders, and something about them was not right.

"Supercan, Bucket, Lily Belle," he said. "*Where's Camp-bell?*"

Just then Tiddley began to act strangely. He would dash off as if he were hunting for something, and then he would come back and sniff all around Sparrow, who was still sleeping. Then he would come to Andy and put up his nose and whine or bark. After he had done this twice, Andy suddenly realized what was wrong. *Dot was gone too!* Dot and Cambell! They had vanished completely.

Andy leaned over and shook Sparrow's shoulder. "Where's Dot?" he asked.

Sparrow sat up sleepily. "Go away," she said. "I haven't finished sleeping. And Dot's right here beside me where she's been all night."

"No, she isn't," Andy said. "She's gone!"

"Dot gone?"

"Yes."

"Where?"

"I don't know."

Now Sparrow was wide awake and scrambling to her feet.

"And Campbell's gone too," Andy said. The two children looked at each other with worried eyes. Then they looked at the robots, but there was no use in asking them. There they sat with their medals gleaming, and whatever had happened to Dot and Campbell they must have seen, but they would never be able to tell it.

"Lily Belle, try to tell us," Andy begged. "You're the only one who knows how to talk."

But Lily Belle only burst out laughing, "Ha! ha! ha! Ho! ho! ho!" and then she went on to yodel. At such an early hour of the morning the sound of yodeling was weird and frightening in the shadowy woods. The birds stopped twittering in the trees, and presently Lily Belle herself fell silent, as if she could not bear the sound of her own cheerful voice.

All too late Andy began to think what a dear, sweet child Dot was after all, and how fond he really had become of her. And he thought of Campbell, who had never done anyone any harm and who had been the only tin man not to get a medal.

"What shall we do?" asked Sparrow.

"We'll have to look for them. They can't be far away."

"What if Dot has fallen in the river?"

"I don't think so," Andy said. "Look at Tiddley now. I think he has picked up a trail."

It was true that Tiddley seemed to be very excited about something. With his nose close to the ground, he was starting up the trail toward the berry patch. Sometimes he ran back, as if he had lost the scent, and then he started forward again. He whined and wagged his tail with eagerness. They could see that he was doing his best.

"The berry patch!" Sparrow exclaimed. "Dot wanted to go there yesterday. She remembered where we got the berries. Maybe she went there to get her breakfast."

"Berries!" Andy said, and under his breath he added, "Bears!"

The two children began to follow Tiddley up the hill as fast as they could go. They had forgotten the three robots. Since no one told them to do anything, they continued to sit beside the fire, and at every five-hundredth *ding* of his bell Supercan added a piece of wood to the blaze.

"Dot must have told Campbell to come with her," Andy said. "Otherwise he'd still be sitting there with the rest of them, like a dummy."

"I don't know, Andy," Sparrow said. "Sometimes I think that Campbell has more sense than any of them. You just didn't give him ways to express himself. He looks dumb, but I don't believe he really is."

It seemed a long way to the berry patch this morning. The woods were damp and chilly, and night shadows still lurked under the trees. The children went as fast as they could, but Tiddley ran faster, and suddenly they heard him barking shrilly.

"Do you think he's found them?"

"He sounds more scared than happy," Andy said. "It's as if he had some wild thing up a tree." They ran on faster after that, and the rising sun was just beginning to light up the berry patch when they reached it.

Across the open space of the clearing, they saw Dot. She had evidently found enough berries to stain her face with juice, but she was not picking berries now. She was standing very still, and her eyes were wide and frightened. She was not even crying, but just standing still as if she could not move away. Sheltered behind her stood Campbell, and both of them were gazing at a big black bear who towered over them.

Tiddley was barking and dancing back and forth around the bear. The bear stood on his hind legs and showed his teeth in an angry snarl. He had been going after Dot, who looked plump and tasty to him. But now Tiddley's arrival had spoiled his breakfast.

Before Andy could shout or do anything helpful, he saw the bear strike Tiddley with a heavy paw. The blow sent the little dog flying into the bushes, yelping with pain.

Now that he was free of the dog, the bear turned his attention again to Dot. He towered above her, and he was about to seize her when there was a sudden flash of shining tin between the bear and the baby.

"Campbell!" Sparrow gasped. "It's Campbell!"

The robot had flung himself between the bear and Dot, and the bear's big paw struck the robot's middle with a sharp sound of claws on tin. A look of great surprise crossed the bear's face. He was reaching for something soft and juicy, and his claws had struck something hard and shiny instead. He began to back slowly away.

Now Andy and Sparrow were both running toward the bear and shouting and waving their arms. The bear saw them for the first time and turned quickly and lumbered away into the woods.

By the time the children reached Dot and the robot, Tiddley had come limping and whining out of the bushes. Sparrow fell on her knees beside Dot.

"Baby, darling, are you all right, little Dottie?"

"Dottie a'right," the little girl said gravely. "See poor baby."

At first Sparrow thought that Dot meant herself, and then she realized that Dot was pointing at Campbell. She was not even laughing. Sparrow looked around and saw that Andy was helping the tin man to his feet. The bear's claws had made a great dent in Campbell's middle can and had raked across his face in such a way as to change his whole expression. Half of his baby smile had been scraped away, and he seemed very stern and grown-up.

Andy dusted him off and set him on his feet. He looked at the robot with respect and admiration.

"Great frogs and catfish!" Andy cried. "You are a hero, Campbell! A real hero. You saved Dot's life, and you've grown into a man. Did you throw away that other bottle cap, Sparrow?"

"No," Sparrow said. "I've got it in my pocket. And Andy, it ought to be first class and for extra-extra-extraordinary merit, don't you think?"

"Yes," Andy said, "I do."

Dorinda Floats

There were a number of things which had to be done before they could leave the island. First of all Campbell had to have his medal. That seemed the most important thing to all of them. The children made as fine a ceremony of it as they had made for the other robots.

Andy said, "Campbell, you have done something better than any of the rest of us have done. You have saved a baby from a bear, and in doing so you have got your middle dented in and your face scraped. For this I take great pleasure in awarding you a First Class Medal for—"

But just as he was about to stick the medal to Campbell's

dented chest he remembered that there was no more melted pitch. He did not know what to do next. Everyone paused, and even the robots began to look disappointed.

Suddenly Sparrow cried, "Wait! Just a minute." Out of her pocket she took the tiny piece of Doublemint gum she had been saving. She put it into her mouth and began to chew it very rapidly. "I knew," she said between chews, "if I saved it—it would come—in handy—sometime—and I guess—this is the—time."

When the gum was nice and sticky, Sparrow took it out of her mouth and stuck it to the underside of the bottle cap. "There you are," she said to Andy. "I didn't get all the flavor out of it, but we really had to have it right away."

"Good," said Andy. "Thank you, Sparrow. Now, Campbell, I do, sure enough, award you a First Class Medal for extra-extra-extraordinary merit." So saying, he stuck the bottle cap on Campbell's chest.

Campbell made a polite bow, and he did not hold up his arms to be kissed. That was a pleasant surprise to everyone. After that they were joyful for a short time, as long as Andy thought they could spare from preparations for their journey.

"Now, tin men," he said, "we have one big job to do before we leave the island. Even if our boat works, it will not be large enough to take Daisy and the pigs, and I don't want to be bothered with the hens. But if we leave them here unprotected the wild animals are likely to destroy them. What we have to do is to drive the bear and the foxes off the island, so that the farm animals will be safe until somebody can come back and rescue them."

It turned out to be good fun. Lily Belle yodeled and sang, the children shouted and beat sticks together, Tiddley barked, and Supercan rang his bell. The two largest robots went crashing and beating their way through the brush, followed by the others, making all the noise they could. Before long they were pleased to see the bear and two foxes swimming away from the island toward the distant shore. Now Andy felt satisfied that the domestic animals would be safe until they could be rescued.

By this time the three children were very hungry, and they were glad to have the breakfast of milk and eggs which the hens and Daisy obligingly provided. As he was eating, Andy looked around at his beautiful camp and sighed. There were the wickiup, the ring of stones around the campfire, the log seats on either side. "We might have stayed until snow flies," he said wistfully to himself. He did not say it aloud, because he knew that the idea would upset Sparrow, and now the important thing was to make the boat work, if they could. But he knew how a good camper should leave a campsite. So now he went about tidying everything, and last of all he poured water on the fire so that not a spark was left.

And now he could no longer put off the moment of trying the boat in the water. Sparrow was already at the water's edge, examining it. "It looks good, Andy," she said.

Andy ran his fingers over the pitch. "It feels hard enough. I hope it holds. We'll have to see." The two big robots were there to help Andy turn the boat over and push it into the river. Everyone stood anxiously around to see if the new board and the melted pitch would really make the boat safe for all of them to get in and ride to shore. The river was very calm today, and *Dorinda* just bobbed gently up and down on the surface of the water. The inside of the boat seemed to be perfectly dry. So far, it did not leak.

"First we will put Dot and Tiddley and Campbell in, and see what happens," Andy said. "Hold the boat steady, Supercan. Now, in you go, Dot."

Dot came and held out her arms to Andy and let him lift her in. Today she was just as good as she looked. Andy lifted Campbell in next, and Tiddley jumped in by himself. Still the boat did not leak. Andy began to feel pleasantly excited. "You next, Sparrow," he said. "You and Lily Belle."

Sparrow climbed in gingerly and sat down beside Dot. Andy lifted Lily Belle over the side, and even Lily Belle seemed to be holding her breath. She did not utter a "ha" or a "ho" or a "help! help! help!"

Now a tiny bit of water began to seep along the cracks of the boat, but it was not much. It was not as bad as it had been all summer long when Andy had rowed up and down the river in it.

"It doesn't even leak a little, small amount, does it, Andy?" asked Sparrow anxiously.

"I think we can make it," Andy said gravely, "if Bucket is ready to bail and Supercan to row. I'll steer for shore, and it shouldn't be long until we find a town or village."

The river had already gone down several feet from the high water of the flood, and it flowed quietly. In a few days it would be back to its normal size, and life along its banks would go on as it had before the storm.

Andy was the last one into the boat. He shoved it off from shore and jumped in just as the current caught it and whirled it into midstream.

"Row, Supercan!" Andy shouted. "Row!"

Bucket stood ready to bail, but such a very little bit of water leaked in that he had almost nothing to do. It was an odd thought to have at this moment, but suddenly the idea came to Andy that it might have been quite easy to calk and paint the boat early in the season, if he had ever taken time to get around to it. But now he was too busy steering to waste time in useless regrets. The important thing was that *Dorinda* was mended and would take them safely to shore.

Andy and Sparrow looked at each other and smiled, and Dot clapped her hands. They all felt cheerful and glad to be alive and fond of one another. The robots glistened in the sunshine, and Sparrow said, "Robots are the nicest people! I'm glad you invented them, Andy."

"So am I," Andy said.

"And look how sweet and nice Dot has grown," Sparrow continued. "I guess you won't mind sitting with her after this, Andy."

"I guess not," Andy said. "I might even trust her with the grape jelly now."

So they rode in happy silence for a time.

Sitting in the stern to steer, Andy was the first one to see the spire of the Methodist Church of Riverdale pricking up into the blue sky. He tried to be very calm and matter-of-fact about it. "Sparrow," he said, "look around behind you and tell me what you see."

Sparrow looked around and gave a little scream.

"It's a steeple!" she cried. "It's a church and a town! Oh, Andy, we're getting to Riverdale."

"Didn't I tell you?" Andy said. He had forgotten all about staying in the wickiup on the island until snow flew. Now the thing he most desired was to get to Riverdale and see if he could find his parents.

Riverdale

"Row fast, Supercan! Row as fast as you possibly can," ordered Andy. Supercan obeyed, and the boat skimmed over the water as lightly as if it had a motor to propel it.

Soon the children could see other buildings besides the Methodist Church. They saw the town hall and the fire station and the Woolworth store. Then they could see the dock at the river's edge, and there were people standing on it.

The people on the dock had evidently noticed the boat that was approaching so rapidly, and they seemed to be excited about it. A shout of welcome floated out to the *Dorinda* while it was still far out on the water. Andy and

Sparrow shouted back and waved, Tiddley barked, and Dot cried, "Hi!"

Then they heard someone on the dock shouting, "Call the Buckrams. Call Grandpa Clayton. I think their kids are found."

"Andy!" cried Sparrow. "Did you hear that? Did you hear that?"

"I sure did," Andy said. "Great frogs and catfish!"

As they approached the dock the children could see people hurrying and shouting and pushing others forward. Some people were hastily moving aside to make room. And then, running down the dock with arms outstretched, came Mr. and Mrs. Buckram. Behind Andy's parents came Grandpa Clayton, and he was running too, faster than Sparrow had ever seen him run before. Behind him came Cousin Eva and her husband. They were all there.

Cousin Eva was weeping and saying, "My baby! My baby! Andy saved my child!"

Mr. Buckram was shouting in a loud, proud voice, "I told you nothing could happen to Andy. He's a very inventive boy."

Mrs. Buckram called, "Andy, darling, you've torn your good shirt, and your face is dirty. But I do love you very much anyway."

Grandpa Clayton was too much out of breath to speak, but Sparrow could see his little snowball beard working up and down and tears running down his cheeks, and she knew he was as glad as she was.

The boat came alongside the dock. "Stop a minute,

Supercan," Andy called. Supercan obeyed, and quickly Andy passed Dot up to the arms of her parents. Then he and Sparrow and Tiddley all jumped out. In a moment Sparrow was in Grandpa Clayton's arms, and Andy's mother was smothering him with kisses, and at the same time his father was trying to shake his hand and clap him on the back.

They were all talking at once, asking one another what had happened, and how they had managed to get here, and telling one another how happy they were to be together again. It was a wonderful moment of reunion.

All the other people on the dock were pleased and interested too. In fact everyone was so much interested in the reunion that nobody thought about mooring the boat.

Suddenly Andy remembered the boat full of robots. He would get them all out now and tell everyone how useful they had been. He turned around to look at them, but they were no longer there beside the dock.

"The boat!" Andy cried. "Where is it? Where are my robots?"

All the others turned to look too, and they saw that the current had carried the boat full of robots away from the dock and back into the mainstream of the river. Even worse, Supercan had begun to row again. He was rowing fast, as fast as he possibly could, just as Andy had ordered him to do when they sighted Riverdale.

"But I told him to stop," Andy cried. "You heard me, didn't you, Sparrow?"

"Oh, Andy," Sparrow cried. "You said, 'Stop a minute,'

that's what you said. He obeyed orders exactly. As soon
as the minute was over, he began to row again, as fast
as he possibly could."

Too late Andy began to shout, "Stop! Turn around and
come back! Stop! Come back!" But the wind was in the
wrong direction, Supercan's bell was jangling, and Lily
Belle was singing. The robots did not hear him.

"Oh, my robots! My wonderful tin men!" Andy cried.

"Oh, save them, my darlings!" cried Sparrow. But there
was no boat handy, and in any case no one would be able
to row as fast as Supercan could.

The robots were already headed downriver. Their faces were all turned around, looking backward toward the shore where Andy and Sparrow stood. Supercan's oars were flashing in and out of the water and his bell was ringing, Bucket had begun to bail, Lily Belle had begun to laugh, and only Campbell held out his arms as if he wished to be taken up.

"Can't somebody do something?" begged Sparrow. She started to cry now, and tears ran down her cheeks.

"It's too late," Andy said. "They've gone too far. We'd never catch them."

Grandpa Clayton wanted to comfort Sparrow.

"Don't cry, Sparrow," he said. "They're only tin men, dear. Don't cry for tin men."

"I don't care," sobbed Sparrow. "They're more than tin to us. We love them, don't we, Andy?"

"They saved our lives," Andy said. He kept swallowing and blinking his eyes to keep back the tears. He did not want to be a baby, even a brave one like Campbell.

"Well, there goes my boat," said Mr. Buckram.

"But it wasn't much good anyway," his wife said, "because Andy never got around to calking and painting it."

"We can buy a new one," Mr. Buckram said, and his wife added, "And I guess it was a good thing that Andy spent his time building the tin men instead of mending the boat. He says they saved his life."

The robots were growing smaller and smaller now as the boat went farther away.

"There are lots of little islands at the mouth of the river, Sparrow." Andy said. "The robots don't have to eat, and if they find an island they'll know now what to do to make themselves comfortable."

"That's so," Sparrow said. She had a momentary vision of the tin men sitting on a log beside a campfire. Behind them was a neat wickiup which they had built themselves. The firelight flickered and shone on their tin faces and on their medals. And, if she had not burned herself up getting fire, Lily Belle would be laughing or singing.

"Still I can't help crying," Sparrow said, wiping her

eyes on the back of her hand because, of course, Campbell still had her hanky. "Oh, I'm glad he has it," she thought. "It may comfort him. They were so good!"

But suddenly Andy's face had changed. His sorrow was almost gone. He began to look pleased and excited. Just as the boat full of robots was disappearing around a bend in the river, he had noticed something shiny in the sand at the edge of the water.

"Sparrow, wait!" he said. He ran along the dock and down to the shore.

The shiny thing was half buried in the sand, but Andy pulled and pried and brought it out. It was a bright new can about the size of Campbell's middle part. Andy held it up.

"Look, Sparrow!" he cried. "We can start right out on a new batch!"

"A new batch?" Sparrow said. "Oh, yes, we will. We'll make another batch!"

And so they did.

CAROL RYRIE BRINK bases her very popular books on real-life experiences. The idea for *Andy Buckram's Tin Men* came from reading a newspaper account of a boy in California who had built seven robots out of cans and pieces of tin. Mrs. Brink's two other books for Viking, *Family Grandstand* and *Family Sabbatical,* were inspired by incidents in the lives of the author's family. *Caddie Woodlawn* (Macmillan), the winner of the 1936 Newbery Medal, is also based on true stories, those of her grandmother's childhood.

Carol Ryrie Brink was born and grew up in the college town of Moscow, Idaho. She attended the Universities of Idaho and California and, shortly after graduation, married Raymond Brink, a young man she had known almost since childhood. After their marriage, the couple moved to Saint Paul. There, Mr. Brink taught mathematics at the University of Minnesota, and Mrs. Brink first began to write. Her early stories were solely for the enjoyment of her two children; eventually some of these stories grew longer and turned into books. Mrs. Brink has also written eight books for adults.

In 1954, Carol Ryrie Brink was honored by Hamline University as one of twenty-eight outstanding women of the state of Minnesota. In June 1965, she was given the honorary degree of Doctor of Literature by the University of Idaho. Following her husband's retirement, the couple moved to La Jolla, California. They continue to visit Minnesota in the summer.